MW01103298

THE MONTH
AFTER SEPTEMBER

A NOVEL

TOBIAS MAXWELL

The Month after September

Copyright © 2020 Tobias Maxwell. All rights reserved. No part of this book may be reproduced or retransmitted in any form or by any means without the written permission of the publisher.

Published by Wheatmark®
2030 East Speedway Boulevard, Suite 106
Tucson, Arizona 85719 USA
www.wheatmark.com

ISBN: 978-1-62787-820-3
LCCN: 2020911663

Bulk ordering discounts are available through Wheatmark, Inc. For more information, email orders@wheatmark.com or call 1-888-934-0888.

Direct author inquiries to:
TOBIAS.MAXWELL.AUTHOR@GMAIL.COM

For Melinda Price

Contents

Prologue

My story begins before all the chaos. When the streets of Quebec knew about turmoil but not yet about absolute power. Knew about class struggle and the inferiority that comes from being Catholic peasants, relegated to the serving classes. Second-class citizens who worked the factory floors, who tilled the farmland and cleaned up after the rest of the electorate.

Today, at sixty-five, I speak perfect French. It belongs to me without any qualms, even though I learned it somewhat late in life. That is to say, it was not in infancy that I absorbed its richness. Oh, my mother spoke it to us as children, and we spoke it in the house, but mostly ours was an English household. Like one thinks of a right-handed or left-handed person, where one side is dominant. Rarely are they ambidextrous. The same could be said of our bilingualism.

I wish all of that were incidental to this story, but it isn't.

In Bern, Switzerland, where I spend half my days promoting the science behind innovative medicines, my life lends itself to French, English, or German, as if I had always belonged there. Andres, my American partner, makes love to me in English, even if he is fluent in Spanish, and his heart lies deep in the Catalan of his ancestors. I suppose we are both traitors in that way. We meet in English because it's simpler. It's our Treaty of Versailles without any of the heraldry and the diplomats. Forgetting all too easily the outcome of that failed pact.

When we're in New York and I listen to Andres converse with his parents, I'm reminded of the transgressions we take for granted when we bastardize what our birthrights were—once upon a time—when he reverts to plain Spanish, or when I speak à la française instead of my French Canadian patois. As though it were all a frivolous game ...

1963

The Montreal street on Queen Victoria Monday, that early in the morning, was in a stupor. Reveling from the evening before had added to the lull, as men with hangovers and tired mothers still lay in lumpy beds before the demands of the day and the ongoing celebrations got underway again. The sun had barely risen over the horizon, holding in its mouth the coolness of a May night that lingered on the island.

A man in his early fifties, dressed in work clothes, tugged at the tweed cap on his head, tipping it so that it covered more hair as he walked nonchalantly. He dragged on his unfiltered cigarette as he bent down to tighten his shoelace, the stealth in his squat going unnoticed.

The Armory, not a hundred feet ahead of him,

with its sizeable carved stones and matching turrets, was an impressive structure. The historical location had been chosen for its proximity as well as its connection to Anglo rule. The man studied the stronghold briefly, making a mental note, like he had done a dozen times before. At the mailbox, he carefully slid the package down into the slot via a camouflaged string before walking a few yards away and onto the street, into a car that pulled up as if on his command.

The vehicle drove off slowly. The purr of its engine filled the street with the first of the day's noises until, suddenly, the crashing wail of a bomb exploded, ringing out into the stillness.

1968

The Jamesville Social Hall had very little character to speak of. The utilitarian 1950s architecture, strewn over Ontario towns, was a legacy of the Ontario Tories, in power for over a decade. The tight building lines were plain and functional, as though any froufrou in design would have been suspect—certainly too liberal.

"I heard Trudeau got into hot water today." The woman addressing Jeanine had tight brown curls that looked permed, if the dried texture of the strand ends meant anything. The two women were seated beside each other, part of the gaggle of New Democratic Party volunteers. Bob Mercier and his wife, Jeanine, both in their mid-forties, had signed on to the NDP campaign the week before.

"What'd he say now?" Jeanine asked, scarcely listening as she spotted her husband gesture for Peter, their son, to come over. The dark-haired fifteen-year-old moved from the end of the table, where he was stacking the counted-out pamphlets for their riding. His father leaned in and whispered in his ear before gently pushing him on. Jeanine could see Peter's disinclination as he went off to help a girl at the table opposite them.

"Oh, something about that queer bill of his from last Christmas? Remember that one?"

Jeanine did. "Ah, not that again," she replied, though she wasn't that interested. "What's he gonna let them do now?" she added rhetorically, watching Peter make his tentative advance. When the attractive girl beamed at his approach, Jeanine experienced the kind of relief only a mother with a teenage boy could feel. Though her son wasn't tall for his age, she was buttressed by the fact that he had a charming disposition that went with his placid nature, two gifts that came from her side of the family, she thought.

Peter glanced back. The glint in his father's eyes felt like a paternal thumbs-up. "Hi," said Peter, thinking his voice had actually cracked when he heard his tinny overture above the din of the crowd. Any ego boost marshaled by the girl's smile deflated in an instant.

The June humidity had shattered all records in the eastern part of Canada that year. The Ottawa Royal Canadian Mounted Police headquarters were bustling over the teletype memo just received from Montreal. Irene, the secretary in charge of collecting and forwarding, had rushed the message up the line of command. Back in the secretarial pool, she noticed the human electricity all about the place. The buxom widow had never seen so much commotion in such short measure. She reread the copy of the all-caps memo still in her hands: DEATH THREAT CONFIRMED. FLQ SUSPECTED. PRIME MINISTER TRUDEAU WILL NOT CANCEL APPEARANCES. MONTREAL AWAITING INSTRUCTIONS. Saying it aloud now made the event more real. She peered at the women around her who had paid her attention, each very aware of the hazards the Front de libération du Québec might pose. "Montreal must be up in arms."

Their no-nonsense supervisor, a Mrs. Witkin, by merely clearing her throat, gave the clerical workers a stern reprimand, sending each of them back to their Dictaphones and typewriters.

*

In Montreal, Sergeant Megan sat patiently at the

desk of Superintendent Higgins. Cigar smoke saturated the room. "It's getting late," Higgins said. The senior officer puffed, letting the smoke curl around his tongue before releasing the flavor. "We should have heard back from Headquarters by now."

Megan, only a decade younger than his superior, had his years in the army that predisposed him to think otherwise. SNAFU—Situation Normal: All Fucked Up—was the order of the day when the pressure was on. He nodded, at the ready, in abeyance to the powers that would provide them their mandate.

"They'd better give the okay for plenty of backup." The doubt in Higgins's voice carried a soberness rarely expressed on the job.

That seemed to embolden the underling. "Do you think they'd mind if we rounded up half a dozen FLQ'ers?" Megan asked, his way of making small talk. "You know … just the more radical ones. The activists. Play it safe?"

The fringe element of French Canadians, adamant to free Quebecers from their English oppressors, had rattled around Megan's brain for years and likely carried more weight than it should have—if Higgins had been a betting man. The older officer thought he understood Megan's objectives perfectly well. Still, he shook his head reluctantly.

The implication—that those cowboy days were behind them.

"Suit yourself, sir. But when they have themselves a dead prime minister on their hands ..."

*

The Pine Avenue apartment furniture was sparse. An ancient, beat-up couch and a round coffee table, which once coiled massive cables for the telephone company, were set up in front of a portable television set. A ceramic ashtray in the center of the table overflowed with butts and ashes. Claude, Remi, and Noel were nursing beers, while Claire drank coffee, all captivated by the prime minister's speech at a gathering in a midtown hotel. "The fundamental question of the campaign is our future as a united country." Pierre Elliott Trudeau's enunciation always resonated as he reached for rhetorical hearts. "Our home, *chez-nous*, is not just the province of Quebec. It's the whole of Canada."

"Fucking traitor," Claude yelled as he shut off the set. The twenty-five-year-old's temper did not bode well for their cause, Claire thought, loathing this latest tension amongst them. She went to the window and counted backwards from a hundred, lest she spark another round of bickering.

Jean-Louis Lalande snuck in from the back entrance through the kitchen. He made absolutely no sound on purpose, testing his mettle at every turn. The tall nineteen-year-old projected intensity, as confident of himself as any man twice his age. His striking features—dark and handsome, with eyes the color of emerald green, whose golden hue at the center of the irises made for a formidable presence.

Remi stood up. "And ...?" he asked their intruder.

"It'll reach." Here in their group, as much as everywhere else he might have endeavored, Jean-Louis's bravery commanded respect. He took Remi's cigarette and dragged on it.

Claire, already in her early thirties, could feel the relief from her younger cohorts. She left her perch at the window and crossed over to kiss him on the cheek, a token of goodwill.

*

The Saint-Jean-Baptiste Day festivities got underway early that evening in Lafontaine Park. The Monday had all the hallmarks of a long weekend, as revelers mixed with anti-Trudeau agitators who held signs and chanted over the police cadre guarding the location. The shouting came from everywhere, interspersed strategically through the crowd of Liberal supporters who were clearly in the majority.

"*Trudeau au poteau!*" screamed a man at the top of his lungs.

When the prime minister and a group of dignitaries walked onto the reviewing stand, the hostility turned passionate, as defenders and demonstrators began to tussle. "*Pouilleux, débarrassez-vous de vos poux*," railed one of the activists. Some protestors threw objects—a tomato, some raw eggs. The elected officials took their seats, disconcerted but unable to break with the minister's stance, which was nothing short of unflappable. The brawling gave Jean-Louis the cover to get into position.

The makeshift plastic bottle, filled with urine, sailed past Trudeau, as two RCMP officers dived to protect him. Undeterred by the chaos of the melee, an obstinate Pierre Elliot Trudeau regained his determination to lead. The prime minister conferred with his bodyguards, who let him resume his pose on the same seat as before. Glaring at his fellow politicians was Trudeau's way of being gracious to a fault. The rankled minions followed in his footsteps so that Trudeau could smile victoriously to the wild applause from the crowd.

*

Later that night, back at the Pine Avenue apartment, Noel and Jean-Louis sat on the couch, smoking a joint. The news broadcasting black-and-white images of the picketers at the parade hardly showed the anger that had galvanized at the park. Jean-Louis leaned into Noel to examine his bruised forehead. "They really hit you bad." Noel moved away, preventing him from rearranging the bandage.

Jean-Louis admired the man, who had every reason to be jaded yet wasn't. At thirty-four, Noel was the eldest of their cell, recruited for the cause by an uncle, long dead at the hands of unknown assailants. "The bastard's lucky; I'll give you that." He took the joint from Jean-Louis, aware that they were lucky too, not getting arrested during their mini-uprising.

"For now." Jean-Louis's expression reflected a calm, along with his resolve.

1970

The Mercier bungalow was one of the first to be built in the eastside subdivision of Jamesville. The ranch-style, at the height of its popularity when the house was constructed in the mid-fifties, was situated just past the empty fields and wooded areas that once belonged to the cotton mills. In the years since the closure of the factory compound, the east end had expanded, in spite of the dilapidated buildings that marred the scenery. The once-busy industrial site, which had included a trolley and tracks that carried manufactured wares to the train station north of the town, had afforded terrific childhood adventures for Peter and for his older brothers before him. It's where the Mercier boys and their friends had learned to use their knives and pellet guns, gaining valuable independence, scouting the patchy woodlands. Overgrown now and poorly kept by the township, the landscape had been reclaimed by rabbits and rodents and clowders of feral cats that had relocated after the industrial turmoil of a century. On hot summer days, the backyard views of the open acreage gave the house a country atmosphere, like it was their own private garden.

On the cusp of turning seventeen, Peter had filled out but not grown much taller—a trait from his father's side of the family. His chestnut-brown hair, worn well below his collar, had an auburn sheen that complemented his dusky blue eyes. He shuffled into the kitchen, half asleep.

"You came in late again last night." His mother was at the sink, rinsing the breakfast dishes.

Peter poured himself a bowl of cereal from one of the two boxes left for him on the kitchen table. He went to the fridge for milk and dribbled some over the flakes, preferring dry to soaked. "I did?"

Jeanine ignored the artful response. She gazed out the kitchen window above the stainless steel sink, to the lawn that was overgrown after a week of continuous rain. "Your dad expects the grass to be cut by noon." When Peter gave no answer, she added, "He wants you to help him canvass too." She knew the answer behind his uncommunicativeness;

disliked even more the nagging, but she had no recourse. "Peter?"

Her son got up, threw the remaining cereal into the side sink, and ran the garbage disposal before exiting by the back door. Jeanine cleaned up the few items that remained on the table and returned the cereal boxes to the cupboard. She had just retrieved the dustrag from under the sink when she heard the lawnmower humming in the backyard. "*Merci, Jésus*," she said, peering heavenwards.

* * *

The Jamesville Social Hall had not changed much since Peter had last been there. The space tonight was filled with inebriated partygoers, celebrating the success of their silent auction—the New Democratic Party fundraiser from earlier that evening. At the far end of the room, just below the stage, Jeanine and her son were manning the snack side of the refreshment stand. They had not been particularly busy, enjoying the lulls as they came, even as the room temperature rose with the degree of intoxication. She monitored Peter while he made change and deposited cash in the drawer. "You tired?"

"Of all this?" He examined the room in one fell swoop. "Yeah."

Jeanine had asked a simple question, expecting a yes or no. His overarching rejoinder took her by surprise. At nearly seventeen, her youngest, was not a risk-taker. She was thankful of that, in spades. Having raised two other boys, with the middle son, Eddie, a finicky personality from the start, she knew she was blessed with Peter's affable temperament. With Bob Jr. successfully placed at the paper mill and Eddie gainfully employed out in Vancouver, she had her sights set much higher for Peter, which was why she paused to consider how best to respond.

"Don't let your father hear you say that." She looked around to ensure her husband was out of earshot. "I know this can be boring." She had wanted to encourage Peter, but as soon as she uttered the sentence, she grasped it had not reached its mark by far.

"Why didn't the others have to do this?"

The idea of Bob Jr., but especially Eddie, doing any of this with them almost made her laugh. "We weren't political back then," she said, hoping to placate, "when your brothers were your age. There was no need. Everything was just fine back then."

"Everything's fine now." He had hardly spoken when the two heard Bob Sr. over a rowdy communal harrumph in the background nearby.

"The Official Languages Act was nothing, I tell ya." Bob's beer quota for the party had clearly been surpassed as he uninhibitedly provoked. "Wait and see." As if the year-old federal law could be anything more than diving in the weeds for policy wonks.

A man dressed in a flashy three-piece suit, too young to truly grasp the relevance of the law, wangled closer to Bob. "You're paranoid, Bob. That's your problem." A few people joined in tenuous laughter.

Jeanine thought of interrupting, knowing how volatile and argumentative politics could be when mixed with alcohol and testosterone.

"Paranoid, eh? Laugh, you'll see. These FLQ'ers aren't gonna be satisfied with French as an official language," Bob griped, taking the last swig from his bottle of beer. "And the NDP's gonna have to stand up to all of those extremists when the time comes." Bob felt queasy from the buzz of too many beers. "*If* we want to keep Canada the way it's been."

The man put an arm around Bob's shoulders, intent on comradery. "Well, I'll give ya this much, Mercier. Pierre Trudeau and his Liberals aren't the answer. We all know that. We can agree with the FLQ on that one." The group, circled around them, cheered, lifting up glasses and bottles of beer to toast.

* * *

The oft-repeated line that Jamesville Central

Collegiate was the best high school in town was tongue in cheek, given that JCC happened to be the *only* high school. That their secondary school options were limited was never lost on the students enrolled there.

The main structure, built at the turn of the century, had a glass addition constructed for Canada's centennial in 1967—a glaring feature that clashed from every angle with the more classical lines of the original building. The older section's façade, made of Queenston Quarry limestone, had prestige, precisely because of the link to the famous quarry. A Jamesville mayor in 1903, with connections to the Niagara region, had cinched a generous deal for the town.

The school's architectural charm was mostly in its frontispiece, with heavy stone bands carved in the Ionic columns on each side that left more than a fleeting impression. No one could enter through those doors for the first time without some mild appreciation for history, even if only because of its stone. The 1967 centennial addition notwithstanding, the municipality's years-long struggle with the province to achieve heritage-preservation status had gone unheeded.

Peter walked down the west hallway to the end of the corridor, aware that he had only minutes before the start of band practice. He could hear the muffled instruments being played in the private, soundproof rooms. The occasional door opening and closing let out snippets of music—the oom-pah of a tuba, the shrill of a piccolo that traveled out into the hallway—a reminder to everyone that this area was the domain of musicality. Peter, not being a musician, felt awkward every time he went in their vicinity.

He entered the spacious room, the tiered rows of which were scattered with music stands and students with instruments. In the oboe section, he saw his buddy Ryan, seated next to Denise, his latest romantic interest. Ryan noticed him and mouthed, "One sec." He sloped forward towards Denise and her friend Marilyn, who stopped wetting the reed mouthpiece on her oboe. The teenage girls giggled as Ryan walked down one level and over to Peter.

"Marilyn likes you," he told Peter. His matter-of-fact attitude made the innuendo seem like it was common knowledge.

"She does?" Peter was dubious, but when he glanced over, he saw Marilyn smile his way.

"You're comin' with us on Friday, right?" His friend's hesitation irked him. "Shit, Peter." Ryan knew his chances with Denise were solidly more realistic with Peter as wingman to entertain Marilyn. Being weighed down by a third wheel was unacceptable to the junior.

At just six months older than Peter, Ryan O'Hara

was tall, where Peter was short; Ryan, who was on the lacrosse team and dabbled on his electric guitar and whose jaw showed a five-o'clock shadow by three. With a hairy chest and arms, his dark blondness was in sharp contrast to Peter, who shaved only every other day and then only on his chin or where stubble appeared on each side of the indentations under the nose, the philtrum that accentuated the Cupid's-bow shape of his upper lip. They had met by a quirk of fate at an early gathering of the chess club in the seventh grade, when both boys had joined, only to drop out a month afterwards on the exact same day, disenchanted by the slow pace of the game.

"It's not my fault," Peter said, fully recognizing the important role his attendance played in Ryan's love life. "Dad's got us signed up for something," he added, acutely aware that his options were few.

Ryan's sense of battle had been raised. "Does he know you don't agree with that NDP stuff?"

"I agree with it. Some of it ..."

Ryan had been fighting this skirmish for over two years, ever since his best friend's father had joined the local political scene. "You like Trudeau. The Liberals, remember? You said so in debate class last week."

"That was just a position," Peter said, knowing it was a bald-faced lie. He liked Trudeau in spite of his father's indoctrination.

"Convinced me," Ryan admitted, less puzzled than impatient, realizing band practice would get underway soon, and he too would have to leave. He pretended to pace, without actually traveling much.

"Yeah, well ... in my house, we're NDP. What can I say?" Peter stepped away, not wanting to belabor the point.

"Pete. What about Friday?" Marilyn had moved towards him.

Peter turned. Her carefree proposal made him blush. He smiled back, knowing his modest act communicated commitment. "We're on," he answered her without an ounce of contradiction.

That night, his elder brother Bob Jr., his wife, Sandy, and their three kids were invited to dinner. The talk of cutbacks at the mill kept the conversation away from politics throughout the hors d'oeuvres. Jeanine had barely sat down to begin the main course, too preoccupied with her grandchildren. "Mrs. Mercier, your meal's gonna get cold. I can handle this." Sandy took over the reins. She cut and modified Robbie and Diane's portions on their respective plates.

Jeanine did the sign of the cross and recited grace to herself, followed by a second sign of the cross. The religious gesture went unnoticed, as everyone's silence acknowledged varying degrees of agnosticism.

"You still working on that extension in the back?" Peter asked his brother. He was seated next to his nephew, Stephen, their eldest—distracting the kid with a game of footsies so that the boy would eat without any prompting.

"Doin' the inside. You wanta come over and help on the weekend?"

"He can't," Bob interrupted. "He's helping me."

"I can't Friday." Peter hoped he could cross the great divide between his wishes and his dad's without commencing a scene, making the statement quite fast, followed by a gobbling of meat and potatoes.

"What's up?" Bob Jr. asked his father. "What are you doing on the weekend?"

The patriarch was not about to give in or give up his claim so easily. He stared at his youngest. "And why not Friday?" he asked, assuming it was a crucial school activity, now that Peter was in his junior year.

Peter toyed with the lies he could come up with. Did he dare try to fabricate from whole cloth? The lure of living dangerously enticed him, but a promise made to Ryan—which was half true, made the most sense. His answer, "I have something to do," sounded as lame as he knew it was. He wondered how other teens navigated these pitfalls, thinking he might be deficient.

Jeanine's stomach growled from acidity; indigestion always followed when arguments trolled the dinner table. "We're volunteering at the NDP headquarters," she offered to no one in particular, as though making a friendly announcement on the PA system at their local mall. She was too exhausted for political squabbling, and her eating more food would be a waste now. "Peter's been—" she began to elaborate, when she was interrupted by her other son.

"You still supporting those socialists?" Bob Jr. asked. He was incapable of fathoming his father's latest aberration—the NDP representing radical alternatives to Liberals like himself.

Bob Sr. knew the direction this was going in, a trajectory laid squarely for collision. "You got a better choice?" he challenged, like a programmed train on a set of tracks.

"Trudeau," Bob Jr. declared, knowing the antipathy it would create.

"That son of a bitch?" The expletive came out with apoplexy, which occurred when anyone dared mention the prime minister's name in Bob Sr.'s company. Said without rancor—or forgiveness, for that matter—for the man had not done anything to him personally, it was one folly in a life that was generally rational, a fealty to anyone but Trudeau.

Peter rose from the table. "I've got homework." He took a few steps towards the bedrooms.

Jeanine stood up. She was aware that he was

leaving for fear that her husband might put the kibosh on his request for some Friday night social time if he stayed any longer. "I made a nice strawberry short-cake," she said, knowing it was Peter's favorite.

Peter hated missing out on the dessert, his mother's specialty. He could almost taste the fresh whipped cream. "I'm not that hungry. Ryan and me ate some fries at the mall." How easily lying was turning out to be!

Diane, his four-year-old niece, rushed after him. She grabbed at his legs like he was an escaping amphibian. Worried that his father might use the presence of the extended family to manipulate him somehow, Peter reached down and picked her up.

"Honey, don't bother your uncle Peter," her mother politely called out. "He has work to do."

"It's okay, Sandy." Any excuse not to study quadratic functions was fine with him. "She can comb through my rock collection while I do my math." Peter was convinced that leaving the table now, under the cloak of homework, had given him a critical edge. He faked butting foreheads with Diane, who loved to rough-and-tumble with her uncle. The girl squealed happily. "You wanta look at those rocks on my shelves?" The prospect excited the toddler, no end.

* * *

The September evening was balmier than usual, which partly explained why the foursome were outside the arena, enjoying the bright moonlight, taking advantage of the weather to toke behind a salt shed. The arena parking lot stretched out towards the darkened baseball field, where a group of drunken boys were tossing empty beer cans. With a piece of two-by-four as their bat, they sent the aluminum flying, landing one in Peter's direction every now and again.

Each time the side doors opened and closed, ear-splitting rock music would blast into focus, compliments of the live band inside the arena. Then Peter or Ryan would duck over to the side to make sure no cops or security guards had come out to prowl. "Beats stuffing envelopes, right?" Ryan said as he returned.

Peter laughed. He exhaled and passed the joint to Marilyn. In the far distance, one of the beer-can boys had bent over, his retching heard in glorious color. "I wonder what the NDP folks have to say about dope." The joint came back his way, and Peter took a pass. "Too ripped," he confessed.

Ryan toked long and hard before handing the reefer to Denise. "Peter, you oughta ask your dad that." The smoke escaped his lungs against his will. "Just like that—hey, Dad, ya think the NDP might legalize pot for us?" He popped a Life Savers into his mouth to settle his cough. "*That* should keep him from dragging you with him all the damn time."

Denise offered Peter the joint again. Muddled as he was, he took it.

"Or maybe not," Ryan added in his stoned haze; that his advice could backfire on his friend had just dawned on him.

"My parents vote Conservative, I think," Marilyn said before toking on the last remains of the roach. She coughed from the combustion of paper and the pop of a marijuana seed. "What are your folks, Denise? They're not Liberal, are they?"

"Anyone who's for the French, right?" Her English was heavily accented, the only one in the group who was irrefutably French.

"So they must support Trudeau, no?" Ryan saw Peter frown, objecting to his inference. "What?"

"It's not so cut-and-dried like that," said Peter, familiar with the intricacies of his own clan.

Since Denise had not paid much attention to politics, she was tentative. "I ... I don't know, you guys. They're private about that," she admitted.

"Well, it's not the NDP; that's for sure." Ryan's knowledge of politics was matched by his self-confidence.

Marilyn could see the boys were raring to argue. "Why is your dad working so hard for the NDP anyway?" she asked, wanting to deescalate any tension. "Does he intend to run for office? Is that it?"

"His dad hates the French—that's why!" Ryan had lit a cigarette, and he spit out some phlegm from too much dope-coughing.

"No, he doesn't." Peter addressed Denise. "My mom's French." He said it as though his aim was to make her feel more at ease.

"And *Mercier*—what's that?" Ryan scoffed. "Sounds French to me too." He understood the politics of language better than his companions, how it could rile Peter, but he was too blitzed to care.

"Dad's half French." Peter's rather superficial grasp of his family history proved inadequate when it came to defending it. He could see Denise was only semi-attentive. "My dad never really bothered with the language. His mom was British." He could hear himself talking, hear the weakness in his reasoning. "It wasn't too important. Not back then, I suppose. Not like today." Peter had pieced together snippets over the years, mostly from what wasn't talked about—the reticence when questions were asked and only answered partially. Being stoned made Ryan's query profound all at once, which is why Peter blurted, "That makes me—what? Two-thirds French?"

"*Tu parles pas français du tout?*" Denise's tone implied censure as much as sadness if Peter conceded to her that he didn't speak much French at all. She took out an emery board from her purse.

"Not really. I get bits and pieces. I can usually follow along."

"Yeah, sure you do." Ryan laughed.

Denise could not hide her disappointment. "Your poor mom." She got busy with the troublesome hangnail, using a nail clipper. "How does she stand it?"

"The old man must give her what she wants." Ryan nudged Peter in the ribs.

"Hey! That's my mom you're talking about."

The teenagers jostled for position, bumping into Marilyn, who dropped her cigarette on her chest. She screamed, seeing the lit embers on her scarf. Denise pushed away the boys, coming to her rescue. "Guys, geez."

* * *

Jeanine Mercier was sitting alone on the sofa in the living room. The house was pitch-black, except for the lamp beside her that provided just enough brightness for reading. She heard Peter's footsteps as he walked onto the back porch. She looked at her watch, knowing Bob would not approve of the hour. She put the French romance novel down on her lap.

From the darkened kitchen, Peter could see his

mother's silhouette. "Shit," he muttered to himself. *How stoned do I look?* he wondered. He took off his shoes and headed towards her. "I know it's past my curfew," he said, convinced that he could pull off a conversation.

Unlike Bob, her sons being home safe and sound was more important than the hour. Jeanine raised her palms. The implication was that this wasn't a battle she wanted to pitch.

Peter relaxed, appreciating his good fortune. "Not sleepy?" he asked.

She shook her head and lifted her novel as a reason for staying up. "You had fun?"

"Yeah."

"Who were you with?"

"Ryan."

"I assumed that." She smiled. "Just you two?"

"And Marilyn. And Denise."

"Don't think I know those names."

"Uh ... Ryan's been hanging out with Denise. Marilyn's her friend."

"Denise—is she French?"

"They're both French. Or, Marilyn's mom is French. I think she said that." Peter was reminded of the earlier debate over politics. "Mom, how come none of us learned much French?"

Where seconds before she had been youthful and engaged, his question reduced her appearance to a tired slump. Jeanine placed the novel on the side of the sofa and picked up her pack of Player's that was next to the ashtray beside the base of the lamp. She lit one. The duality of simple and complicated was never easy to tackle, she thought. She signaled for him to sit beside her. "Your dad said you kids needed English. This wasn't Quebec." When she spoke, she heard how harsh the sentence came across. She had meant to be conciliatory.

Where before Peter's curiosity had been piqued, there was now a hint of umbrage. "You didn't mind?" he said, like an offense had been done to him.

Jeanine saw where this was leading, a blame-Bob sort of moment of which she didn't want to partake. "I was young. I had to get married." Her own father's and mother's outrage—the combination of premarital sex with all of its inherent complications, made worse by the fact that Bob was an Anglo through and through, with a negligible connection to the Catholic Church—had made them reject their only daughter outright. "You know, Mrs. Mercier was the only one who accepted our situation—me."

Peter could see remorse in his mother's eyes, too adolescent yet to understand the emotional calamity it entailed. "I wish I'd known Grandma Mercier longer."

"Yeah. She was something, all right." The kindness her mother-in-law had shown her from the start had been a godsend, but Jeanine knew how entangled that kindness was with how she acqui-esced too often with Bob. "A gentle force," she said to Peter, choosing not to elucidate on how the British mind-set, with their live-and-let-live practicality, had usurped her strict French Canadian upbringing, inadvertently letting go of her roots without realiz-ing the impact on her children.

"And Grandpa Mercier? He didn't care?"

"The Merciers didn't feel the need. Some spoke French. His aunt Eloise—"

"She the one who married the Belgium fellow?" Peter had only met them once when he was in grade school.

"Married *and* divorced. That was another first your grandma never fussed over." Jeanine sipped the last of her tea. "But everyone just spoke English when we used to get together."

Peter got up from the sofa. "I need to pee real bad." He leaned in and kissed his mom on the cheek. "Good night."

"Peter ..." He was almost out of the living room when he turned around. "Don't ask your dad what you just asked me, okay?"

"Ma, it's a free country," he said, his mood mer-curial, like a typical teenager. "I'm part French too, ya know." He took off in a huff towards the family bathroom.

* * *

The following afternoon, Peter had compensated for his broken curfew by agreeing to help out with NDP tasks. He listened to the women gossip as he folded letters into envelopes. His mind seemed on hold, lagging behind the to-and-fro, an effect from the previous evening's partying. One of the women, an elderly matron Bob admired for her prodigious stamina, took a stack of completed mailers from Peter. "It's heartening, seeing young people take an interest in politics."

The urge to rebel came over Peter before he knew what had hit him. "But don't you just love Trudeau, though?" His disastrous words were out before he could retract them. The disquieting hush, with his father only a few feet away, made Peter get up and leave the room.

Outside, Bob marched towards their car. Peter tried to keep up with his angry pace. "What's the big deal?" he said, knowing his sarcasm had flopped miserably. "It was just a silly joke."

Bob had reached the car. He tried to open the door when his keys dropped to the ground in a pothole. "Son of a bitch." He flailed the murky water with his foot, hoping to shift the key fob to the side, but the power of his anger made them move farther under the car. The thud of Bob slamming his fist on the front hood made Peter jump.

"I'll get 'em," Peter said.

"Don't!" His father's command acted like a delay mechanism for Peter. "*I'll* get 'em."

Peter watched his father squeeze under the car to fetch the keys. "This is so stupid," he said.

His words had hardly been uttered when Bob jumped upright, giving the impression of a force pulling him upwards, so fueled was he by rage. He grabbed his son by the shoulders, the dirty water dripping onto Peter's coat. "Stupid, huh? I work with these folks. Here. And at the newspaper. This is a small town. People know who you are in this town. Did you ever think about *that*?"

All Peter had wanted to imply was that the Liberals had something to say too, but he kept his mouth shut. His father wasn't that much taller, but Peter felt suffocated by his proximity. He could smell the coffee on his father's breath.

"You turning into a Trudeau lover? Is that it?" Bob's expression was severe.

"What if I am?" Peter was contemplating not getting into the car when his father opened the door. He knew that challenge would be met with more resistance than he cared for, so he sat down compliantly but couldn't quite let go. "This is a free country, last time I checked."

His father's silence as he drove out of the parking lot was perfectly acceptable to Peter.

*   *   *

The Ministry of Defense building in Montreal had been newly renovated that summer. The brass plaque displayed at the front entrance, denoting the historical significance of the site, reflected the fall sunset as the security guard opened the locked door to let out a senior officer. "*Bonsoir.*"

"*A Lundi, Monsieur Raymond.*"

The prominent official had managed to reach the sidewalk, when the patter of his footsteps on that clear Friday evening was eclipsed by the detonation of an incendiary device. Glass, masonry, and stone flew in all directions as sirens rang out through the rubble of blasted-out windows.

*   *   *

Jeanine and Peter sat on the sofa watching the breaking news that had interrupted the broadcast of a movie. The destruction depicted by the footage of the Montreal bombing was alarming.

"They're crazy," she said, lighting another cigarette to steady her nerves. The blackened debris from the blast left nothing to the imagination. "When are they gonna stop with all this craziness?"

"When they get what they want," Peter answered. He rose to get a soft drink. "A free Quebec, it looks like," he added, standing at the refrigerator.

"What do you know about freedom?" Jeanine remembered the hardships of World War II like they were yesterday. "People are better off today than they ever were." She couldn't fathom where Peter was coming from but could see he wasn't as bothered by the radical tactics and was troubled by this. "*We* certainly are," she said, wanting to affirm everything she believed in, hoping it might persuade him to alter his opinion. They heard the sound of the back door opening. Mother and son exchanged glances. Jeanine got up and went to greet her husband. "There you are. I kept you some hot supper. You look beat."

Bob walked past them on his way towards the bedroom. "I ate at the plant." They had been typesetting a revised addition of the Saturday paper, working out the angle on the latest terrorist bombing. "I'm pooped," he told his wife. He caught the newscaster discussing the FLQ on television. "Hey, Peter, there's your Liberals for you." His slurred speech suggested more than just a couple of beers after work. "You can thank your pal Trudeau for all that." Bob waved his hand in the general direction of the television. The whole lot of them could burn in hell, as far as he was concerned. What had been the point of fighting a world war, he thought, if this is what it brought them to?

*   *   *

The Saint Lambert fourplex where Mrs. Lalande lived had been built in the 1920s. Apart from the general wear-and-tear, the first-floor apartment had scarcely changed through the decades. The parquet floors, with their intricate woodwork, had lost some of the sheen perhaps, especially where heavy foot traffic had worn down the pattern. And the linoleum in the kitchen, which had been replaced sometime in the fifties, had yellowed with age. But the tiled bathroom, a stylish black-and-white design, still managed to impress, with its claw-footed bathtub and old-fashioned pedestal sink.

Mrs. Lalande's fifty-seven years evoked someone older. A drunk these last ten years, her state of inebriation had made her susceptible to all that came with being plastered day and night. Laconic when sober; lethargic and glib when drunk. She was at the kitchen table when Jean-Louis came in from the back bedroom he used when he was home. "How long are you going to stay this time?" She played absentmindedly with her disheveled gray hair, tightened the sash on her shabby housecoat, waiting for the unanswerable. Jean-Louis poured himself a cup of coffee from the pot on the stove. His brain concentrated on a hundred things. "You're just like your father."

Her son seemed offended, then puzzled. "That all depends," he teased.

Agnes Lalande laughed, as though he had intentionally told a joke. "On what?" She shoved the local paper over to his side of the table and pointed at the black bold-lettered headline: FLQ BOMBS MINISTRY OF DEFENSE. "On who gets killed next?" The indiscernible infected her barb, making additional words between Agnes and Jean-Louis redundant. Mrs. Lalande fumbled for the bottle of bourbon that sat next to the jars of marmalade and jam. She poured herself another stiff drink.

*　*　*

The Montreal coffee shop that morning was crammed. Jean-Louis and Noel were devouring the last of their bacon-and-eggs breakfasts in a booth at the back. They had been unusually quiet throughout their meal, until Jean-Louis's questions came up. The older man, who knew the ropes, had half expected the concern. "It has to be that way. Right?" He wasn't whispering, but both were conscious of their sur-roundings. Noel vetted the booths next to them before he emphasized, "We can't know—anything."

The sweeping statement had Jean-Louis regret the inanity of his query. "I know. I just thought it would be different. That's all." He was already berating himself for having probed in the first place.

Noel inspected the bill. He took out his wallet and an envelope. "Everyone's gotta do their part. Every-thing counts." He reached over the table and gave Jean-Louis the thin packet. The younger man slipped it inside his coat pocket without missing a beat.

"It's all inside there?"

"No, we thought we'd turn it into a scavenger hunt! Make it more fun for you." He got up with the bill and tousled Jean-Louis's hair. "Don't forget your toque. It gets chilly out in the sticks."

* * *

Denise's house, located on the outskirts of town, was on the border between the catchment area for Jamesville and the rural district of Unionville, as far away from Jamesville Central Collegiate as a student could legally reside. The Georgian-style center-hall design was set in the country, with views of fields and pastures from all sides. The other houses that lined the road at acre intervals only emerged at night when their lights turned on.

Denise came up from the basement to answer the doorbell. "Who drove you?" she asked.

"My mom," Marilyn blurted out like there might be shame involved for Peter. When she looked his way, she could see he was too taken by the carved wooden staircase that crowned the stately hallway to care who had done the driving.

"Great house," Peter said.

Denise was accustomed to that reaction. The oak woodwork and the imported European paneling were exceptional features that never failed to strike a note with newcomers. "It was built by one of the original mayors of Jamesville," she said, sounding more like her mother every day. She took their coats and showed them the way. With no parents in town, the octane level was supercharged, which they noticed as they reached the bottom of the basement stairs. Denise felt the energy coming from the high schoolers gathered for her party. "What can I get you?" she asked. She took them over to the custom-built bar, a replica of a Victorian tavern, replete with memorabilia.

"Beer okay?" Peter asked Marilyn.

Denise had opened them a bottle each when Ryan jumped into the mix. He put out his hand, as if holding a gem in his fist. "Here. You can thank me later." He waited for Peter to present his palm and then doled out a few tiny pills onto it.

"What's that?" Peter's curiosity was aroused.

Ryan leaned into Peter and Marilyn. "Acid."

"*Acid*? Oh, not for me." Marilyn recalled Ryan's coy excitement from AP history earlier that day. "Is that the surprise you were talking about this morning in class?"

Ryan grinned in agreement. "You sure?"

Marilyn lifted her beer, clarifying her intent that *that* was the only buzz she was up for.

Peter's gaze had not budged, as the lure of the rough-hewed purple pills gave him pause. "Are you—"

Ryan plopped one into his mouth. "I took one already about a half hour ago." He did a fluid movement with his hand in front of his eyes and smiled like a toddler would at seeing a duckling fly. "Whoa, fuck ..."

Peter rolled the pill between index finger and thumb. He swallowed the acid without much thought behind his action and swigged back his bottle of beer to ensure the drug had passed to his gullet.

*

Five hours later, the party had mellowed to a close. Ryan and Peter were standing on the sidewalk, admiring the night sky—stars that appeared to be waltzing fluidly, compliments of the acid. "I don't remember this sidewalk," Ryan said to Peter.

"It's been there forever, you dodo." Denise was on the driveway, smoking a cigarette. "We're not totally out in the country. We have buses too, you know." She indicated the shelter a half block away.

"Listen, Ryan, I gotta get home." Peter knew flouting his curfew again would get him grounded. "You're way too wrecked to drive me."

"I don't have to stay over, Peter." Marilyn had just returned from using the bathroom. She took Denise's cigarette and dragged on it. "Why don't I call my mom?"

The idea of being on a hallucinogenic while having to make idle chitchat with Marilyn's mother scared Peter senseless. "No," he said, pondering his alternatives when Ryan barged in. He put his arms on Peter's and Marilyn's shoulders, propped against them like they were a swing about to give him a go.

"Am not too stoned. Stoneded. Stoneded. Stoneded," he repeated, pretending he was his own echo, using a downbeat to make it more lyrical. He gawked at the sky again and began to produce clucking noises while twirling around in circles, sending Peter and Marilyn in opposite directions. "We should fly you back home, Peter."

"Cool." Peter buttoned up his fall jacket and went over to Marilyn. "It was fun tonight." He kissed her on the cheek, unsure if more was warranted. "Hey, later. I'm gonna take the bus."

Marilyn had never spent time with anyone on LSD. "You're sure you're okay?" The boys made the experience seem appealing and frightening simultaneously.

"I gotta get home. I'm pretty fucked up."

"You're sure you can manage?" Marilyn peered at Denise for assistance, but her friend was too drunk to care.

"Not really," he said with a shrug. He was too short on cash for a taxi. Too zonked for any interactions with adults that knew him. What choices did he have? "Where's the bus stop?"

Denise pointed to the bus shelter again, while Marilyn snuggled up beside him. "It's so far to your house. All across town. What if you miss the last bus?"

Peter considered the possibility. "I don't know. I'll flag a ride with the Greyhound bus. There's a last one that goes along Thompson Road. My dad takes it coming back from Kingston when he travels for his job. I think I've seen it before. I don't know. I'll figure something out. The walking will do me good." He pecked her on the lips to make amends. "Call me in the morning. See if I'm still alive."

Marilyn poked him gently on the upper arm as he took off. Peter could hear the three of them quibbling about ordering pizza as they disappeared inside the house. At the bus shelter, the schedule inside the glass case informed him he was out of luck by a good half hour. He started walking, fast at first, then slowing down, as his imagination got the better of him.

The wind blowing against the trees, the leaves falling to the ground, the brightness of the moon assailed him and scrambled his thoughts. At times paranoid, Peter would peek around to see what was behind him, only to laugh at the silliness of his fears. He told himself there were no monsters, but the perception that there *might be* kept him quiet for the next few blocks. At the fourth intersection, it dawned on him how far past his curfew he was. This lateness would be difficult to explain. He turned onto Thompson and stuck out his thumb, hoping a friendly driver would pick him up.

He had been walking backwards, making up games in his head to kill time, when he saw the Greyhound bus driving his way. As it neared, he could see the destination sign MONTREAL and signaled wildly for it to stop. Peter ran up the stairs and stumbled, just as he neared the driver. "Ooh, sorry. I'm ... I'm okay." He apologized, then found himself laughing self-consciously. He pulled himself up, just as the driver turned on the lights.

Peter's angle was of an impossibly elongated center aisle. He could see passengers in every seat, some sleeping, others staring back at him for the needless delay. "How much?" The driver had not answered when Peter added loudly and deliberately, as if he or the bus driver might have been partially deaf. "How much to get me to the other side of Jamestown?"

The driver looked at Peter with a grin, mimicking his ambled speech. "A. Buck. Fifty."

Peter gave him the change and walked down the aisle of the crowded bus. At the very rear, he saw two vacant seats and veered for the one next to Jean-Louis. He was about to sit down when the lights shut off, and the bus leaped back into traffic. Peter lost his balance, fell onto Jean-Louis's lap, and burst out laughing. "So sorry," he said, composing himself, sliding back into his side of the seat.

"*C'est pas grave.*"

Peter was aware that the acid was playing tricks with his hearing. "Uh, I only understand French a bit," he said, wading into fraught terrain. "What did you say?"

"No big deal." Jean-Louis had been preoccupied when the bus stopped, still half daydreaming when

Peter tumbled onto him. "A bit?" he said, holding in a yawn. "Better than most English."

"Oh, I'm not English." Peter marveled at why he had uttered such a claim. "I mean, I'm two-thirds French."

Jean-Louis's laugh made Peter uncomfortable. "What part of you's French? Your head or your heart?"

The high-schooler found the question perplexing. He glanced at the stranger, whom he presumed was French Canadian, and noticed for the first time the attractive angularity of his profile. He felt a pull that he hadn't quite defined for himself yet. "I never thought of it like that."

The streetlights, flashing in and out at intervals into the darkened bus, created staggered shadows. Their effect was impossible to ignore. Peter struggled to stay focused—wanting, needing to be lucid. Jean-Louis picked up on the boy's altered state almost right away. He teased Peter by moving his upper torso, imitating a floating rhythm, then laughed when Peter shook his head and shivered. "*Ya quelqu'un qui est gelé*," he said.

"I'm not cold."

Jean-Louis was even more amused. "It's *joual*. You know ... Quebec slang? It means you're stoned."

"Oh, shit. Is it that obvious?" Peter incanted a

silent prayer for his mother to have gone to bed by the time he reached home.

"Yeah." The Montrealer scrutinized his companion more closely. Who did he have here, he wondered. "How old are you?"

The question was unexpected. Peter stalled before answering. "I'm ... gonna be seventeen in a few weeks."

"When?"

"October tenth. Why?" Peter thought of asking if he wanted to come to a party for his birthday but grasped it would be the acid speaking, rather boldly, on his behalf.

"No reason." Jean-Louis faced forward again, thinking about his next move, strongly suspecting that he was in no position to make one. "So ... have you decided what part of you is French?" he asked, tongue in cheek.

"Is it that important?"

Jean-Louis turned sharply towards Peter. "Is fucking important to you?" He could see Peter startle. It was in his eyes that reflected the light from outside. "What? You don't like fucking?" The end of his question was asked in a whisper.

"Yeah, of course," Peter murmured. "Of course I do."

By now, Jean-Louis had turned and placed his

back to the window so that his knees brushed against the side of Peter's leg. The French speaker sized him up from head to toe, as though thinking of something elaborate to wager. "You've never done it, have you? *Tu peux me le dire.* I keep secrets very well."

Peter liked this impromptu diversion immediately. "Tell *me* a secret," he deflected, feeling game for anything now.

"Trying to trick me, *hein*?" Jean-Louis paused, thinking of the best answer. "Okay, I'll tell you something that's better than a secret. Even my mother doesn't know." He gestured for Peter to lean in. When he did, Jean-Louis met him halfway so that his lips were close to Peter's ear. "I like younger men."

The meaning disoriented Peter momentarily. Seconds elapsed while he tried to figure it out. Weren't they basically the same age? Or was he being duped? He was ordering his thoughts when the lights inside the bus came on.

"Downtown Jamesville. Last stop in Ontario." The driver's announcement over the speaker seemed to redefine the boys' situation temporarily. Peter quickly sat back and began to get up.

"Well, this is my stop."

Jean-Louis had not made up his mind about Peter, but he was bored. And the boy's innocence was almost magical in its intensity. "Is it?" he asked pointedly. He thought he had heard Peter say to the driver that he wanted to get to the other side of town. "This is just downtown, right?"

The awkwardness was as painful as the cold outside was bitter. "Oh, yeah," Peter muttered. He had paid to go farther; getting out at this location made no sense at all in this weather. "I just ... need to use the can." Peter mimed "one second" and dashed into the restroom directly next to their seat.

The light automatically turned on as Peter slid the lock sideways on the door. The bulb flickered before staying on in a pale shade of off-white. He stared at his clammy skin in the mirror; saw how messed up he was. His pupils bulged with dilation. Was his pallid hue an hallucination? He splashed water on his cheeks and reached for paper towels, only to find the container empty. He retrieved sheets of toilet paper and wiped his face with them. He giggled aloud when he saw himself in the mirror again. The wet scraps of cheap, waxy-thin paper stuck to his skin and chin stubble, resembling a shaving exercise gone wild.

Almost as an afterthought, he opted for a leak. He had just unzipped and begun urinating when the bus moved again. He straddled himself solidly, one hand holding on to his member, the other to a side bar designed into the wall. He could see urine missing the toilet altogether and had to wash his hands all over again before exiting. When he closed the door, he caught sight of Jean-Louis. His expression was unmistakable. Peter could see he was keen for him to join him again. He was still wiping his fingers against his pants as he sat down.

"So ..." Jean-Louis had shifted once more, sitting with his back against the window to make some room.

The man's engaging smile left Peter feeling powerless. "I don't know how we got into this, uh, conversation—"

"You said you were two-thirds French."

"No, not that. No, the ... the 'fucking' part." As soon as he had spoken, Peter glanced around to make sure no one was within hearing range.

"Oh, that. Well, let's see. *Ah oui, j'me souviens.* You wanted me to tell you a secret. So, I told you the next best thing.'

"Why me? I'm not...like that, you know."

Peter's seat companion paused to redirect the exchange. "I'd say it's not your head or your heart that's French."

Peter laughed. "What's left? My hands and feet?"

"*Non, mon gars.* Your soul. Your soul's French. I can tell. With the right influence—who knows what you could do?"

"The right influence? That sounds—"

"*Quoi*? What?" Jean-Louis asked, a bit defensively.

"You're not one of those radicals, are you?"

The statement, made on the fly, had Jean-Louis do an about-face. His whole demeanor changed as he realized the major tactical error on his part. Peter immediately picked up on the transformation. As the bus came to a standstill at a red light, Peter could see how near they were to his drop-off. "Do you have something to write with?" he asked.

Jean-Louis heard the rushed pace to the question. His puzzlement, as he watched Peter stare up front, was as much panic as infatuation. He tilted sideways, against the boy, to ascertain if there was anything up ahead that spelled trouble for him.

"I have to get off soon. I have to let the driver know." He observed as Jean-Louis retrieved a matchbook and pen. Peter scribbled down his Jamesville address. "Write to me." He leaned over Jean-Louis to reach for the bell cord above the window. "Doesn't matter what," he said. Jean-Louis's hands steadied his torso so that he wouldn't fall. In the aisle, Peter stood with his two feet firmly on the ground. "I am French. A lot more than you think. Will you write?"

Jean-Louis was incredulous at the rabbit hole he had dug for himself. How had he broken the golden rule of his cell? Anonymity above all! He glimpsed at the matchbook cover, then at Peter's suppliant gaze, and read softly, "Pierre Mercier," his French making the proper names sound exquisite.

The bus had come to a halt. "What's your name?"

The man's hesitation made Peter gloomy without comprehending precisely why. "Uh ... Jean-Louis," he said, powerless to stop himself.

"You'll write, Jean-Louis?" Peter wasn't sure he had seen correctly but the tall, handsome stranger had nodded unmistakably. Peter ran to exit the bus.

*   *   *

Noon had just come and gone when the doorbell rang at the Merciers. Jeanine checked to see if any car had driven up their driveway. "Hi," she said to the young woman at the door.

"Hi. I'm Marilyn Sauvé, a friend of Peter's. Is ... Peter in?"

"I'm afraid he's still sleeping," Jeanine confessed, disliking the admission that she had let her son sleep in like that. "A late night?" she asked, eager for an answer.

"It's our fault. Me and Denise." Marilyn understood that a son on acid was surely not what Peter's mother ought to worry about. "He stayed behind after the party to help us clean up the mess. I think he missed the last bus." Marilyn hoped her fibbing was a one-off.

Jeanine left Marilyn seated in the living room while she went and knocked on Peter's door. "Peter?" When there was no reply, she gently opened the door. Low snoring, like a cat's unbroken purring, could be heard. At his bedside, she nudged his shoulder. "Honey, are you okay?" There was no response at first, so she nudged him more firmly. "Peter?"

"Ugh." He tried to sit up but fell back against the headboard, wasted from the might of his first acid trip.

"Someone had a bit too much to drink. You know I don't like to see you like this."

Peter's eyes adjusted to the absence of hallucinations, saddened by the loss of the heightened reality. He considered his mother's appearance a dream until he grasped that it wasn't. "Ugh. What time is it?"

His mother moved around to the window and opened the curtains. "It's past noon. You have a visitor."

A vision of Jean-Louis in their midst rattled Peter. He sat up, assuming the best and worst. "A visitor? Who?" He sprang to his feet in his briefs and was jumping into a pair of jeans left on the floor when his head let up. Thinking he might faint, he sat back down, rubbing his stomach, making a mental note never to mix alcohol with LSD again. "Where ... where? Here?"

Jeanine walked over to the door she had closed for privacy. She was suspicious now but couldn't pinpoint why. "That girl. The one you talked about a few weeks ago. Marilyn. She's in the living room." Her son's body odor had drifted all the way to where she was standing. "Maybe you should take a hot shower before you come out? You don't want to scare her away. *Dépêches-toi*. Hurry."

* * *

Mount Royal Park blossomed in the fall. The verdant foliage, too overlooked in the final weeks of summer, preened like a peacock now that the variegated colors of October were on display. Noel and Jean-Louis walked down a secluded path into the cemetery. "You knew it was going to be like this." Noel's guard was on high alert as he monitored their surroundings. "That was the way it was planned. From the very start. You can't switch your assignment now. That's crazy." Noel inspected the sheet of paper with the map Jean-Louis had drawn for them during his trip. He placed the sketch inside his pants pocket, next to his switchblade.

"I know. I know," Jean-Louis repeated, struggling

to explain why his mood was careening like it was. *What* is *wrong?* he thought.

"Are you bored with us? Is that it?"

"No." Jean-Louis realized it was more complex than mere allegiance. "So ... you'll contact Remi's uncle if you need the farm." There was no question there. "The layout fits our needs. It's out of the way. They'll never think to go that far—into Ontario."

Noel contemplated the exploits about to commence, the importance of his leadership now more delineated than ever. He put his arm on Jean-Louis's shoulder and gripped it—half massaging, half imploring. "No one knows anything from now on. Okay?" The weight of his body pushed fully against Jean-Louis. "We just have to watch the news. We've done what we were supposed to do."

Jean-Louis freed himself from Noel's tactic. His encouragement, if that's what it was, gave the impression of intimidation. He stepped towards one of the graves and read the ancient dates of the deceased, unconsciously, like he would the tombstone of a relation. It was that history all around them that inspired him to speak up. "It's not enough, is it? It doesn't feel like it's enough. My father would—"

Noel approached and whispered in his ear. "Forget your father. For once!"

He shifted Lalande in front of him, and they

strolled in silence until they had reached a fork in the pathway. "You had your chance last year. When the camps split up. We all did. We all made our choices. Now it's up to fate." Noel extended a hand and pulled him towards him, once Jean-Louis accepted it. "It's not finished; it'll never be finished until we have our independence."

The acolyte—for that was how Jean-Louis felt in Noel's presence—listened but heard only slogans. "Our independence," he repeated with a hint of sarcasm. "*Vive le Québec Libre*." The two walked away in opposite directions.

* * *

"Sorry I'm late," Peter offered upon arrival. Bob and two other volunteers were sorting fliers at the Jamesville Social Hall, debating the new language the NDP had incorporated into their donor literature. "I had to do some research in the library." He held up his science textbook. "A biology paper."

"No problem, son. It's pretty dead here anyway." Bob snapped a rubber band around a packet and placed the bundles into a cardboard box. "Maybe we should just call it a day."

A volunteer came in from the kitchen. "Guys, come here. Quick." The man's agitation made them scurry. They could hear the radio as they walked into the kitchen area. "It's on all the stations. I just heard it."

"Just a short while ago, we are told"—the CBC announcer's tone was more solemn than usual—"armed gunmen kidnapped James Cross, the British trade commissioner, from his home here in Mount Royal."

The group listened to the details from Redpath Crescent in Montreal. Minutes into the broadcast, Bob spoke over the radio. "Now it's gonna start. We've got war on our hands. It's what I've been saying all along."

Peter saw the scowl coming from his father. He kept his head down, riveted by the particulars of the James Cross kidnapping.

* * *

School, the following day, had an electric air, as everyone talked of the FLQ and Quebec independence. The halls were crowded after lunch with students heading for their afternoon classes. A senior on the varsity football team walked past the vice principal, wearing a black armband.

"Take that thing off immediately." Mr. Chumley's bark was nothing if not intimidating.

"Why? I have a right—"

Before the student could finish stating his

opinion, Mr. Chumley grabbed the athlete by the arm. "I'll show you your rights." He tore off the offending symbol without much effort. "The next time you want to make a statement, why not try getting an A on a test for a change. Now get to class!"

Peter and Marilyn had come into the hallway towards the end of the altercation. The fuming student brushed up against Peter, whose books fell to the ground. They heard him mumble, "Sorry," and watched him skulk away.

Peter arrived home after school to an empty kitchen. He could hear the television coming from the living room. "What's for dinner?" When there was no answer, he made his way into the next room. His mother was alone, glued to the news broadcast. "Did they find him?" he asked.

His mother shushed him, pointing to the TV.

"The exhaustive search is ongoing ..." Peter recognized the anchorman but did not know his name. "Tension mounts as the worst is feared. There is still no decision on whether the government will air the FLQ manifesto as a condition for the release of British Trade Commissioner James Cross."

"A manifesto? Wow, I wonder what it says."

Jeanine would have none of that. "Does it matter what it says?" She shut off the television and aimed for the kitchen as she finished her thought. "It comes from violence. What good can it do now?"

Peter followed right behind her. "Maybe we need to hear it first. Maybe there's info we don't know about. Why else would people go to the trouble of kidnapping someone?"

His mother stopped in her footsteps at the refrigerator. "*Mon Dieu*. What are you saying? You're scaring me, Peter." She took out some leftovers in containers and went over to the stove. "How can you think, even for a second, that kidnapping could ever be right?" She put food into various pots and turned on the burners. "Set the table."

Peter did as he was told. He took plates and cutlery from the cupboards and drawers. "It's not like they're going to hurt him. They just want to be heard."

Jeanine hadn't grasped how naïve her son was until now. "Of course they're going to hurt him. They always do. The government can't let them get their way."

Peter took out glasses and cups. "Then it's the government that's to blame."

The two heard the car coming up the driveway. "For God's sake, Peter. Don't say this kind of stuff in front of your dad. He'll flip out if he hears you say stuff like this."

Peter lifted his arms to the air, as though he had been sentenced for life. "Of course not. We can't ever say anything in front of him. God forbid we upset the old man." He ran off to his bedroom, slamming his door behind him.

*   *   *

The hallway alcove at the far end of the science wing was packed. Students were huddled around a transistor radio, listening to the CBC broadcast of the FLQ manifesto.

"We have had enough of promises of work and of prosperity, when, in fact, we will always be the diligent servants and bootlickers of the big shots, as long as there is a Westmount, a town of Mount Royal, a Hampstead—all these veritable fortresses of the high finance of Saint James Street and Wall Street. We will be slaves until Quebeckers, all of us, have used every means, including dynamite and guns, to drive out these big bosses of the economy and of politics." The English dubbed over the French announcer's words came off as didactic, making the declaration eerier to the listener. "We live in a society of terrorized slaves, terrorized by the big bosses, Steinberg, Clark, Bronfman. Next to these, Drapeau the Dog and Trudeau the Pansy are peanuts. We are terrorized by the Roman Capitalist Church."

Audible jeers came from the crowd. Marilyn nudged Peter as she noticed Mr. Chumley fast approaching them. She grabbed Peter to make a run for it up the stairs. Too late.

"Who's supposed to be in class?" The vice principal's voice reverberated. "You're not all seniors here." As students tried to walk past him, the bulwark of authority blocked their path. "Not so fast. Everyone. Down to the office. All of you. Now!" His commanding girth, along with his height, tended to dispel willful disobedience.

* * *

"I don't know why I let you do this," Denise said, not tentative as much as skeptical. It was the following evening, and Ryan had persuaded her and Marilyn to drop acid.

Ryan squinted in the low lighting; she did seem quite discombobulated. "It's Pete's birthday. Come on; lighten up." He played the air with his fingers, pretending to be a musician strumming an angel harp. The four echoed oohs and ahhs at the display of connecting traces left by his digits.

"I thought your birthday wasn't till tomorrow, Peter." Denise sat up on the sofa, hoping her breathing would be less arduous with her back straighter. She stretched her neck, wanting to clear her air pipes and expand her shoulder blades. "We should have done this tomorrow, *non*?"

Being under the influence again was like revisiting a cherished friend, Peter thought, concluding that the rec room's décor was less inviting tonight, for reasons he could not explain. "My folks are having this meal thing. Can't go out on my own birthday!" He was slumped down, practically falling from his seat. "I need to move."

Denise turned around, surprised by his assertion. "You want to leave home? *Bien, arrête.* You're way too young for that."

Peter laughed. "What are you talking about?" Was she *that* stoned? "I just need to move from this couch." He stood and shook out his legs. "I can't feel my feet. I hate when this happens." He went to the center of the room, stomping his left foot to get the pins and needles to cease. When they did, he surveyed his surroundings like it was his first time there in that basement. "Who wants to dance?" He returned to the sofa and pulled Marilyn towards him, but his lack of strength or her unwillingness to budge caused her to fall down against the other couple.

"I have a better idea." Ryan kissed Denise passionately, ignoring Marilyn's close proximity. When Denise did not protest, he made a play for her breasts. Marilyn slid over to the other side of the sofa at first, then rose and sat down on the stuffed chair. Her smile at Peter went undetected, the teenager too ripped to make the connection. He walked over to the record player. The first chords of "Band of Gold" rang out from the speakers as he began to dance. He reached for Marilyn, who allowed herself to be pulled up now, her disappointment never registering with Peter.

*   *   *

The family members were seated around the kitchen table, set for a birthday meal. "He knew it was going to be at five, right, Mrs. Mercier?" Jeanine appreciated Sandy's support more than she let on, ever cognizant that her daughter-in-law was sensitive to any tension when it came to Peter and his father.

"Of course he did." Bob stirred from his chair. "It's his darn birthday." He retrieved two beers from the refrigerator and gave one to Bob Jr. "He should never have stayed over at Ryan's. Those two are getting into trouble."

He had only begun to express his concern when Peter rushed in from the back porch. He looked tired, and his hair was a mess. "Sorry. Ryan's car ran out of gas. We had to walk to the gas station, then back to the car."

"That's all right." His mother came to his rescue. "You're here." She took his jacket and kissed him on the cheek. "Happy birthday, Peter. *Assis-toi*."

Peter pointed to his hands and excused himself for the bathroom. When he returned, he had on a fresh, clean shirt, and his hair had been combed and parted. "This is great. Bobby. I didn't know you were all gonna be here."

"You woulda been here earlier for them; is that it?"

Jeanine gave her husband a dirty look. "Bob, can you pass me a roll, please?" Before Bob could reach the bread basket, Peter snatched the wicker dish and served his mother.

At the end of the meal, Peter opened his presents. The last one came from his father. Those gathered around waited with bated breaths, aware of how fragile the peace was between them. "*Canadian Politics: A History in the Making.*" Peter read the book's title aloud. "Gee, thanks. Maybe I can do an extra-credit book report for—" His sarcasm was cut short by the ringing of the phone.

Bob picked up the receiver. "Thanks." He hung up and ran to the living room to turn on the television. Everyone, including the grandchildren, followed on his heels.

Bob fiddled with the channels until he got to the CBC on the dial.

"On the same day that was to see the negotiated release of Mr. James Cross, a second kidnapping has taken place. Just over four hours ago, the Quebec minister of labor and immigration, Mr. Pierre Laporte, was abducted."

"Those bastards!"

"Honey," Jeanine eyed her husband, "not in front of the little ones." Sandy rounded up her brood. She led them back to the kitchen with a nod of thanks to Jeanine.

"So who are you gonna blame for this one, Peter?"

His father's accusatory manner did not sit well with Peter. "Maybe if everyone had listened to the people in Quebec a bit more, none of this would ever have had to happen. The NDP hasn't been that—"

"Don't go putting down the NDP. If it wasn't for the Party ..." Bob muted the TV set to hone in on his message.

"Dad, Peter, let's not argue about politics." Their endless conflict was draining. "Not today." Bob Jr. was reminded of Eddie's battles with their father. The lost high school years of acrimony seemed to be repeating themselves here. *So much for Peter being the obedient son*, he thought.

"Why not? Didn't you know your brother here's an FLQ sympathizer?"

"Well, at least I'm willing to examine my own history a bit. I'm not ashamed to be French, like some people here."

"*S'il te plait, Pierre.*" Jeanine had already reached for her cigarettes. "Let's not fight. Not on your birthday."

Bob departed the room in a huff, leaving Peter taken aback, though suspecting a ploy. "Good riddance," he muttered. When Bob swept back in, a sweat building on his brow, he held a letter between his fingers and waved it in Peter's face. "What's that?" Peter asked, trying to see the writing on the envelope.

"Since when have you got friends in Montreal?"

A swelling dread took hold of Peter. In his wildest dreams, he had not anticipated this. A letter? So soon? He flashed on Jean-Louis, seated in the half-darkened Greyhound bus. "Montreal? Since ... uh, since ... a while now. What's the big deal?" He tried to snatch the letter, but his father held on to it tightly.

Jeanine exhaled from a slow drag on her cigarette, upset with her husband's impromptu confrontation. "Bob, we said we'd wait till Monday."

The statement of collusion bothered Peter, and he retaliated with force. "When did it get here?" he snapped. "Since when do you go through my mail?"

His mother moved closer to him, putting a hand on his arm. "It's not like that, honey. Your father and me—"

But Bob would have none of it. "Since people are getting killed and kidnapped; that's when. You think I don't see what's going on here? I know what you're up to. I had a talk with that vice principal of yours at school. You think the FLQ's got a point. He's heard you talking."

"Chumley? He's a retard. Can I have my letter? *Please*?" he insisted, knowing that attitude would not win him any favors with his father.

"We need to know who it's from." Bob resembled a referee, not about to capitulate.

"Dad, is that really necessary?" Bob Jr. had never seen his father this dictatorial, even during his own idiotic days, binge-drinking with his other brother, Eddie.

Bob glared at his eldest son, grasping that he was in a minority in his own home. "Bobby, I'm worried about this." He held up the letter so that Bob Jr. could see the sender's address. "There's no name with the return address. See that, Bobby? Who does that? Someone with secrets; that's who."

The mention of secrets only made Peter blush, recalling Jean-Louis's confession to him. He could see the beautiful face, the strong chin, the curl to his locks. All he could do was deny. "That's crazy."

"Okay, then you open it. Read it out loud. See if it's so crazy."

The fear of what this might reveal was too great. Peter's mind raced with alternate pretexts. He didn't know the man who likely had written to him. He only knew what he thought of him—the abstraction of a chance meeting on acid and hormones. When Peter could think of nothing more substantial, he went with simple obstruction. "No. It's mine. I have a right—"

"And I have a right to make sure you're not getting into any trouble," his father countered. Bob handed the letter to his youngest.

Peter faltered as he accepted the envelope. He could see the Saint Lambert address written in block letters, no cursive anywhere. *What* did *you write to me?* he wondered. Then he became excited at the thought of what might be inside. The exhilaration went to his chest, and he could feel his heart pounding—a pleasant pounding, then not as pleasant, as he imagined his mother's disapproval if Jean-Louis disclosed too much. "If I tell you who it is, can I have my privacy? You don't have to know the details."

His father considered the offer for a second, but his suspicions were too ornery to let this slide. "I have to know what's in that letter, Peter. Both your mom and me ..."

Peter glanced at his mother, beseeching his case. He could see she was resolute. She indicated with a movement of her head for him to listen to his father. With no other recourse, Peter opened the envelope and read the single-page note for all to hear. "*Amuse-toi bien. Les crapauds sont gelés cet hiver.* Your friend, Jean-Louis." Peter held up the page that had three miniature picture stamps of ice-covered toads. They were stuck with a piece of Scotch Tape under the few written lines, coded language that told him to enjoy the drugs.

Bob looked at his wife. "What's that supposed to mean? Who's Jean-Louis?"

"This ... guy who used to go to my school," Peter said, making it up as he went along. "His family moved away to Montreal last year. He always used to make fun of us 'frogs.'"

His family members stared at him, even Sandy, who had returned from the kitchen to take in the drama asked, "He's French, right? Why make fun of his own kind?"

Peter could tell he was being evaluated. "He's like us. French with no—"

Jeanine interrupted by reaching for the letter. "They're cute. I wonder where he got them."

Peter feigned examining them again as he took back the letter. "He probably printed them himself. He was always doing stuff like that in art class." Peter waited. "Looks like he did them with a screen, right, Dad?" he asked, going all in with this gambit.

Bob was unconvinced. "What's his last name, this Jean-Louis fella?"

Peter knew better than to be reckless inventing another unsupportable falsehood out of thin air. He paused again, as though he might just educe the family name. "You know, I can't think of it offhand," he said truthfully, never having learned Jean-Louis's surname. He folded the letter back into the envelope. "Can we have my cake now?"

He went towards Sandy, who was pleased that the commotion had mostly subsided. Only Bob stayed behind, fidgeting with the volume on the television to hear more news about the Laporte kidnapping.

* * *

On Monday morning, Ryan met up with Peter in the front of their high school's main entrance. "I don't want to go in."

"Uh ..." Ryan's first period was his study period. With little to lose, he asked, "What do you want to do?" Peter took out the blotter acid stamps. "Where'd you get those?"

"A friend." A wind came down through the branches of the majestic elms that shaded the front entry. Peter instinctively tucked the stamps back to the safety of his shirt pocket.

"Since when do you know where to get acid?" Ryan's curiosity was heightened at the thought of tripping again.

"Since ..." He produced the letter, enjoying having the upper hand.

Ryan noticed the address in block letters and read the note. "Who's Jean-Louis in Saint Lambert, Quebec?"

Having leverage felt powerful, Peter thought. He shuffled a few steps away. "Come on; let's get wrecked."

*

That evening, Bob and Jeanine were in the living room when Peter entered from the back porch. With no one in the kitchen, he called out, "I'm home."

"I'm in here," his mother answered from the other room.

He walked in, surprised to find his father there. "Dad, you're home early from work." Since Mondays were always late nights due to production meetings, Peter was compelled to ask, "Anything wrong at the paper?"

His mother and father, seated on the sofa, together but apart, made the setting peculiar.

Bob stood and walked towards his son. He studied his face very closely. "Where's that letter ya got the other day?"

Peter shifted uncomfortably. "What letter?"

"Don't be playing games."

Jeanine saw it was already time to intercede. "Now, Bob ..."

Her husband ignored her and continued his inquisition. "How was school today?"

An unwavering doom loomed over Peter. "School?" he said, sensing that his house of cards was about to fall. "Uh, school was—"

Before he could begin his tall tale, Bob intervened. "Don't lie to us! The school called. You weren't there. You ditched. You were doing drugs!"

"Drugs!" The accusation of drug use sounded worse than the deed, Peter thought. He gauged how much outrage he could afford. "What are you talking about?"

His mother rose from the sofa. "Peter, Mr. Chumley had a lengthy talk with us. Some kids told him you had LSD. At school!"

"Those damn toads," Bob exclaimed, oblivious to the absurdity. "They were drugs. In my own goddamn house! How could you, Peter?"

"I ... I really don't know," he said, realizing that he was still too stoned to handle the confrontation. His bravura turned to meekness in a flash.

"You're on those drugs now, aren't you?" Bob said, advancing on Peter so that he actually did come off as crazed and scary.

"I need to go to bed." That he appeared like he might pass out, that his head reeled with subdued hallucinations labored Peter's breathing some. "I'm not feeling well."

His mother took his arm and felt his temple for a fever. "We need to take you to the hospital. Bob, he's on drugs."

Peter reclaimed limb and skull and stepped away from her. "I'm fine. I just need to sleep."

His father stooped over him, impressing upon his son all of his authority. "Oh, no, you don't. You're not sleeping off drugs in *my house*."

The emphasis on *my house* stirred Peter to anger. "Your house? Okay, then. I'll leave. Is that what you want?"

Jeanine quickly stepped between them. "Peter. Bob." She had a mind to push her husband out of the room if it could appease tensions. "Stop it."

But Bob would not be deterred. "No, Jeanine." He glared at his spaced-out son. "He's gotta know that he can't take drugs and skip school. And continue to live in our house."

"You know what?" Rage on acid, for Peter, was a liberating force. "I'm out of here." With that, he moved to the right of his mother. "You happy?" he told his father, conscious that he would have to swerve around him to get by. "I'm tired of all this." Body and mind were at odds as the adrenaline pumped through him. Peter was a few feet past his father when Bob seized his son's jacket. "Let go of me." Peter pulled at his coat. The brief tug-of-war caused the material to tear. His parents' alarm at the turn of events made them both stop, the pause drawn out enough to give Peter the chance to make a run for it.

Within the hour, Peter and Ryan had driven to Denise's. The three were in her basement on the sofa; the boys looking wasted, and Denise, glum. "My parents are going to come down here any time. It's a school night. Peter, you've got to go back home. Your parents are going to be worried." She glimpsed at her watch, then over to the stairs for the ump-teenth time.

"You can crash at my house," Ryan suggested. "I'll tell my mom we have to cram for a test."

"She won't buy that? Will she? We don't have the same classes."

"It's my mom, right?"

Peter knew he had a point. Ryan's father being out of town had its advantages, too.

"What else can you do?"

"I don't know. I thought I'd head for Montreal."

His seating companions peered at him like he had lost his marbles. "With what money?" Ryan demanded.

Peter thought of checking his pockets. He had a ten and two ones. "How much do you guys have?"

"Don't look at me," said Ryan. "I'm broke." The boys did an about-face for some encouragement from Denise.

"Aren't you going to call Marilyn?" she asked, disregarding the monetary request.

"I don't want to upset her. You know how emotional she gets."

No one could argue with that.

When they arrived at Ryan's house, there were no messages from Peter's parents. "You're sure, Mom?" Ryan asked again.

Mrs. O'Hara put down her glass of wine, as if implying, *Really?* "Should they have called?" she asked.

"No. No," Ryan stressed, as a means to pacify her. They slipped away to his bedroom and set about clearing the floor area for a sleeping bag. They had stripped to skivvies and were in their respective beds when Ryan spoke from his higher perch. "You can't go to Montreal."

"I don't want to go back home." Peter moved around in his sleeping bag, trying to get comfortable on the carpeted floor. "They were gonna send me to the hospital. Just because I was coming down on acid."

The two considered the optics and began to giggle uncontrollably. "Shush," Ryan said, sporting a pillow to muffle Peter. "Can you imagine one of those operating room lights going to the back of your eyeballs? Pumping out your stomach, maybe. Ugh."

A shiver went through him. "Talk about a bummer trip!" He put out the bedside lamp.

"This floor's hard as rocks," Peter said in the softest of voices.

"Sorry, Mercier. This bed's too small for two."

"I promise I won't breathe much. I'll stay real thin." He could hear Ryan sighing, moving over to make room for him. Peter hopped onto the cozy mattress without so much as a word.

*   *   *

The following day was overcast, foreboding with its heavy cloud cover. Marilyn ran to Peter as she saw him come up the front steps of Central Collegiate. "Your mom called me last night!"

"She did?" Peter felt terrible about that.

"It was late. She was convinced I was hiding you or something. My parents freaked."

"What did you tell my mom?"

"What could I tell her? I didn't know." The insinuation, that Peter hadn't called her, reverberated some.

"I know I should have called you." Mrs. O'Hara, with the sherry decanter, came to mind. Had she been too drunk to deliver a message? "It was all happening so fast. In real time." He took her hand. "Shit. Sorry. I was with Ryan."

"I know; Denise told me." From the corner of her eye, she spotted Mr. Chumley coming from the administrative offices. "Don't look now."

"Well, well, Mr. Mercier. You decided to honor us with your presence today. What happened? Couldn't get any drugs?"

The teenagers tried not to crack a smile at the adult sarcasm. They started on their way, only to be blocked. "Wait a minute." The administrator addressed Marilyn. "You can leave." He turned to Peter. "So how do you propose getting back into school? Do you have a note for yesterday's absence?"

Peter produced his forgery, compliments of Ryan's penmanship. Mr. Chumley scrutinized the paper, pretending to decode a sensitive, confidential document. "Umm, that's interesting." He folded the incriminating evidence. "You were sick, were you?"

Peter affirmed with a nod.

"You have some visitors." The vice principal directed him towards the front office windows. He could see his father at the counter inside as he drew near. Next to him was a stocky man in a policeman uniform.

*　*　*

Peter's bedroom had never felt as claustrophobic as it did today. In his short seventeen years, he had never been this determined, a doggedness that enraptured him completely. He rushed about, putting clothes in a gray backpack—underwear, T-shirts, and some sweaters. Approaching footsteps from the hallway made him throw everything to the back of his closet, just as his mother entered.

"Peter. There's some soup on the table." Jeanine stood, waiting for a response.

"I'm not hungry." The unspoken only rendered more pain between mother and son.

"He didn't plan it like that, you know," Jeanine said, still at the door. "That vice principal called the cops. Not your dad. It's not your dad's fault at all."

Peter rearranged the coverlet that lay half fallen onto the floor. His gaze directed away from his mother's. He stared at the posters of the Who and Jethro Tull on his walls.

"Your dad's just as confused as I am. These drugs, Peter. We don't know anything about these drugs."

"Maybe it's time you learned about them." Peter wanted to get up, but staying seated worked to his advantage. "It's not a big deal."

His mother's patience was being tested. *"No big deal?"* Her high-pitched inflection showed all of the anxiety cooped up inside her. "You're skipping school. The vice principal says your grades are going to go down if this keeps up. We just want to know who that friend of yours is in Montreal. That's all the officer wanted."

Peter knew his case was tenuous, that sharing more would only aggravate his dilemma—or so he imagined. "I explained it all already. I don't know the guy. I threw that letter away. It's that simple."

Jeanine's intuition told her there was more afoot; she couldn't quite put her finger on it but was compelled to try. She sat on the bed and patted the mattress to get Peter to come nearer. He resisted from his end; stood instead, rigidly, by the headboard.

"Peter, it doesn't make sense. Why would a stranger just send you drugs? You said it yourself; it's weird." She wanted to hone in on Peter's claim that he had exchanged his address on a whim, looking for a pen pal, but refrained.

"Mom, maybe he's a pusher. Maybe he thinks … if I take the drugs, I'll want more. I'll start to buy from him." Peter hated himself for tarnishing Jean-Louis's reputation, but his options were nil. He dug in his heels. "Come to think of it, he did seem like the dangerous type."

Peter's words did not console Jeanine. She smoothed out the coverlet at the foot of the bed and noticed a pair of clean socks rolled up by the dresser. She picked them up, thinking she had dropped them on the floor when doing laundry, and tossed them at Peter. The lighthearted gesture made her son relax.

He juggled the cloth ball up and down in his hand and sat back on the bed. The last thing he wanted was to eat soup. Eating her soup now was tantamount to collaborating with the enemy.

Wednesday,
October 14, 1970

The car's interior was stuffy, reeking of tobacco and
what Peter thought was perspiration and possibly
liquor. The driver, a chain-smoker in his forties,
dressed in an inexpensive business suit, lit another
cigarette. At the top of the hour, the music on the
radio was interrupted for a news brief. The man
turned up the volume.

"An unconfirmed report has just come in." The
radio announcer's deep baritone added drama to
the bulletin. "One of the FLQ kidnappers has been
apprehended. A source close to the RCMP stated
that they suspect the man was directly involved with
the abduction of Mr. Laporte. No further details are
forthcoming at this hour."

Peter glanced at the motorist who had picked him up on the highway just east of Jamesville. Ted, as he had introduced himself, had scarcely spoken, once the distance to their destinations had been conveyed. In his peripheral vision, Peter could see his backpack resting neatly on the seat behind him. He was really doing this, wasn't he? That morning, he had waited down the street from his house, waited for his mother to leave on her errands, so that he could get into his bedroom and retrieve his backpack with the belongings he had thought worthwhile for running away. He had walked north to the outskirts of town to get to the highway, musing on all of the unknowable before him.

Too excited to fret over consequences, Peter studied the man behind the wheel, assuming he was married with children. He checked and saw that there was no wedding band to suggest as much. He hesitated when the offer of another cigarette was made, then accepted. Knowing he would soon be out of money and cigarettes, that beggars couldn't afford to be choosers, the high school truant embraced his new motto.

Outside the car, the dreary skies predicted an early snow. Peter inhaled and exhaled. His eyes went to a road sign that posted forty-two miles to Montreal. Reaching Dorval, the agreed-upon drop-off, brought no more than a grunt on Ted's part. Peter was thankful. The natter of politics to ruin his adventure was not on his agenda that day.

Two more rides and two and a half hours later, Peter got out of a truck and adjusted his backpack. Saint Lawrent Boulevard felt fresh and alive after the mundane of Jamesville. The smells from the Jewish delicatessen in front of him made his stomach growl. He jingled the coins in his pocket, aware that his fortune was just under twenty dollars, along with half a pack of cigarettes. He glanced at his cheap Timex. Two thirty reminded him of how starving he was. He entered the restaurant and ordered a sandwich and soft drink.

As he ate at the counter, contemplating his next move, Peter watched the portable black-and-white television set that was placed above the cashier. The volume was low but loud enough so that he could hear the TV anchorman.

"The man apprehended earlier today and who was believed to have been one of the kidnappers of Mr. Laporte managed to escape only a few hours after being taken into custody."

The rotund woman manning the cash register whistled before resuming her gum chewing. She scratched the hairnet that covered a gray bouffant but not the lacquered kiss-curls at her ears. Her drop-earrings that cascaded the length of her neck made her more eccentric than attractive.

"Isn't that just the craziest thing you ever heard of?" she said.

Peter, who was within earshot of her comment, gave her a quizzical look. "Maybe the cops who were holding him were FLQ sympathizers," he offered, his words traveling far enough to be heard by the customers and employees nearest to him. When he saw the woman openly hostile to that likelihood, Peter chomped the last bite of his sandwich and drank what was left of his Sprite. His mouth was bulging with food as he counted out his money, put the bill on the counter next to the cash register, and scurried out of there in a hurry.

Inside the Metro station, Peter examined the city map and the subway lines. He held up Jean-Louis's envelope to make sure that his instincts were correct. He bought his ticket and traipsed down the flight of steps. Inside the heated compartment, the rubber tires rolling against the tracks whirred as the train cars transferred the passengers from station to station.

At the next stop, an elderly man walked in. When he opened his paper, Peter saw the blaring front page headline: PROVINCIAL GOVERNMENT LOOKS TO FEDS FOR HELP. The escalation struck a chord with Peter. At the far end of the train, a bunch of French high-schoolers began making a ruckus, going from noisy to obnoxious quickly. Though the language eluded him, Peter wondered how their world was managing the chaos; whether they too had any conflict with their fathers and mothers.

* * *

Ryan had placed his dog-eared copy of *Playboy* beside him on his bed, in preparation of foreplay, when the front doorbell ringing made him reassess his plans to masturbate. He heard mumbling and could tell it was his father with another male. He was on the verge of starting up again when his father's imposing voice resonated from halfway up the stairs.

"Ryan, can you come down here? Right now."

He checked the alarm clock on his bed stand. Who came by at night like that? Ryan entered the living room to see his dad next to Peter's father.

"Hello, Ryan." The men appeared in lockstep, standing together.

"Mr. Mercier," said Ryan, keeping it formal, as though this were a job interview and Bob a manager.

"Why don't we all sit down?" suggested Mr. O'Hara, cutting through the tension. They moved onto separate pieces of furniture.

"Ryan, this is real important." Bob's resolve made Ryan sit up straight. "We don't know what kind of man this Jean-Louis is."

Ryan knew that Peter's being escorted out of

school by police the previous day was a false rumor. Marilyn had disobeyed the vice principal and lingered in the hallways to gather that vital intel for them. But running away for real? Ryan had never believed his buddy capable of such rebellion.

"What if he gets Peter in trouble. Peter was real angry last night, Ryan. He's liable to do something stupid."

Ryan reacted with panic of his own. Had he been responsible for this, turning Peter on to acid? The notion seemed ridiculous. But four weeks ago, Ryan would never have predicted that Peter could run away from home. "Mr. Mercier, I swear to you. He didn't tell me anything. I mean, he talked about takin' off for Montreal. But that was a few days back. I just thought he was home today, on account of—you know, yesterday and all." Ryan could see his mother had not brought his father up to speed.

"Ryan, you can't recall the address?" O'Hara watched the boy's dubious expression. "Mr. Mercier mentioned a letter." The blankness coming from his son disappointed him. "You're good with numbers. If you had that letter?"

"Ugh," was all Ryan mustered. He regretted not jerking off earlier. His attention and focus might have been sharper, he thought.

"Try to remember," his father said, feeling an obligation for his son's mistakes.

Ryan struggled, torn between his loyalties to his friend and this abstract duty to respect his elders. "It was a Saint—I remember that much."

"You're right; I remember now too." Bob was so happy for that prompt. His memory of the thin, crumpled envelope was coming back to him.

O'Hara pressed on. "Was that the town? Or the street?"

Ryan gazed down at his bare feet, compelled to continue with what felt like a terrible betrayal of his buddy. "It's the town. I remember 'cause it was like an animal."

Mr. O'Hara went out of the room and returned with some maps of Montreal. The three opened the materials, searching for their hunches. "I never realized how many 'Saints' there are over there. Like Ireland, almost!"

"It's the French for ya." The men had found common ground.

"I think this is it. Yeah, here—Saint Lambert. That's it. I'm almost positive. Lamb."

His father and Bob studied the street listings. "It's a suburb town. On the … south shore, it looks like. Not too many streets, if that's the right place."

"That's right." Ryan suddenly recollected more. "Peter said something about that. He must have looked at a map himself." The fathers stared, skeptical, both thinking he might be playing them for suckers. "Hey, I swear to you; this is just all making sense now. I didn't think about it at the time. I just figured—"

His father adopted a sterner version of himself. "Ryan, what else did he say?"

"It's a tree." He blurted it out. Like a confession under duress. "The street name's a tree ... or was it fruit?" He paused, desperate to visualize the return address he had had in his possession. "Oak, Chestnut—one of those."

Bob rose from the chaise.

Mr. O'Hara did the same from the couch. "Mr. Mercier ... Bob."

Bob had already arrived at the door.

"Bob, you can't travel to Montreal with just that. Let's look at the map some more." He reached Bob, still holding the half-folded map, with Ryan right behind him. He could see the man was undeterred. "Well, you've got those two names, Oak and Chestnut." He turned to Ryan, who had redeployed towards the staircase. "Any numbers?"

Ryan halted in his tracks. "Uh, it was like small, if I remember correctly. I mean, I had the envelope for a while." The admission needed to be disavowed as soon as he saw the dissatisfaction from his father. "It's Peter. He's always losing stuff. He asked me to hold it for him the day we ditched ..." His voice trailed to a murmur as the displeasure showed in his father's eyes.

"How small, Ryan?" his father asked, irritated now by a suspicion of subterfuge by his own progeny. "Two numbers? Three?"

Bob had tied up his coat and scarf and was opening the door. "Don't worry. I'll just drive up and down. The streets didn't seem that long to me."

Ryan recognized that he held some power, but he was also quite unsure of his information. Everything became a blur under pressure. "Two or three. Definitely not four numbers. Almost positive of that."

Bob stepped out onto the porch. Mr. O'Hara stood with him in his slippers and shirt. "Bob, be careful. Montreal's crazy right now. Don't get caught up in the turmoil."

Bob was impatient to get a move on. He was at the top of the veranda stairs when Ryan stretched over the side of his father's shoulder. "It's ten— something." Mr. O'Hara's exasperated sigh sent mixed signals to his kid, but Ryan was unfazed. "Mr. Mercier, there's a ten in the address. I know 'cause that was part of Peter's birth date. He made a comment—something about that." Ryan watched Bob wave goodbye, his back to them. Mr. O'Hara closed the door.

"How grounded am I?" Ryan asked.

The silence, at first, was promising. "Like forever."

*   *   *

Saint Lambert could have been Jamesville, Peter thought, getting off the bus. He had studied the area map at the subway station, traced the outline of a street, memorizing his path forward from either of two bus stops. But for the skyline of Montreal in the far distance, the small-town atmosphere had a familiarity to it. He tightened his scarf around his neck, fixed his toque down over his ears, and headed off.

Ten minutes had gone by when he pulled out Jean-Louis's letter to verify if the addresses matched. With no apartment number to work with, Peter walked up to the front porch with the three doors. He read the four names on the mailboxes. Miller was dismissed automatically. As if his drug benefactor could have an Anglo name! He did the same with the foreign-sounding surname. That left him with a Séguin and a Lalande. He tried out both. "Jean-Louis Séguin. Jean-Louis Lalande." He imagined a young Jean-Louis Lalande responding to roll call in elementary school and selected that one, boosted by the ease of his verdict.

The idea of knocking on the door at this hour of the night did make him nervous. Without the benefit of too much French to fall back on, his one hope was that Jean-Louis would be home, preferably alone. He rang the doorbell to the apartment and heard nothing. When he rang again and could distinguish no stirring of any kind, he knocked once, then more loudly the second time. He could see lights from the front window and a television flickering through the sheer drapes. He tried the door and found it unlocked. "Hello? Anybody home?" With still no answer forthcoming, he redoubled in broken French. "*Est-ce qu'il y a … un quelqu'un là?*"

Peter convinced himself that the man he had met on the Greyhound bus a few weeks prior wouldn't mind if he stepped inside, made his presence known. He advanced into the apartment and saw a woman on a recliner, who appeared fast asleep—he could hear her sporadic snores. The only other sound was the television, the volume of which had been lowered so as to be barely audible. He tiptoed further into the living room, hoping for signs of Jean-Louis to make him more at ease with his breaking-and-entering. He glanced around. The framed photo of a young woman with a man dressed in a Canadian soldier's uniform caught his attention. He had reached the chair and nudged the woman lightly.

Mrs. Lalande stirred, opened her eyes and began to scream. "*Non!*"

Peter promptly pulled back, afraid he had made an egregious error in judgment.

"*Qui êtes-vous*?" she asked, her fear sobering her up from a deep torpor.

"I'm sorry. I didn't mean to—"

Mrs. Lalande rose up from the recliner and tried to run, but the quickness of her movements, along with her fright, made her gag. She bent over, not a yard away from Peter, and threw up on her own carpet.

*

"You can stop that." Mrs. Lalande was at the kitchen table, nursing a fresh drink, watching Peter wring out a rag into a bucket at the sink. "Just put it down."

"I was going to dump this dirty water into the toilet bowl."

Agnes waved him off. When he returned, he sat down across from her.

"There's coffee." She pointed to the stove. "There's some Coke too, in the fridge."

Peter helped himself to a soft drink and stayed by the counter.

Mrs. Lalande picked up the letter he had placed before her on the table. "When did you get this?"

"Last week." The cola bubbles quenched his thirst. "When did you speak to him last?"

Agnes Lalande was gradually reverting to her intoxicated equilibrium. With it, came wretchedness and her distrust. "How come you want to see my son so badly?" She referenced the letter and added, "Pierre?"

The accusatory tone and the use of the French version of his name made Peter defensive, as though he had something to hide. "I don't want to see him so badly. I just … I just thought it would … be—"

"How old are you?"

"Me?" Peter asked, realizing some illegality if he admitted to being a minor. "I'm eighteen."

"*Menteur*!"

Peter knew that meant liar. He was crushed at being found out so readily. He tried to use his French to ameliorate his predicament. "*Je suis dix-sept.*"

Mrs. Lalande laughed. "*J'ai dix-sept.* The way you said it—" She stopped, realizing the phrase was partly idiomatic. "Just memorize the form." The boy's reserve made Jean-Louis's mother curious to find out more about him. "Where did you learn to speak French so poorly?"

"Where did you learn to speak English? It's good." Peter could see that his comment, flattery of a sort, had barely registered. Or if it had, she wasn't about to elaborate for his sake. He filled the void instead by answering, "I'm from Ontario."

Of course, she had known that from the envelope. She reread the Jamesville address; recalled some nexus to her husband in that geographic vicinity. If she had suspected before, now Agnes understood, intuitively, that Jean-Louis was implicated in the latest round of strife. Even in degrees, she felt a duty to protect her son at all costs. Who was this delinquent, anyway? "Jean-Louis doesn't live here," she said, eager to rid herself of the company.

That bit of news came with more complications than Peter had anticipated. "Oh. Where ... where does he live?"

"He doesn't live anywhere." She could see Peter's confusion. "He can't live anywhere. He has to live everywhere." She poured herself another glass of liquor. She doubted this Peter from Ontario was up to any of what might be asked of him. "Is that what you want? Is that why you're looking for my Louis? You want to live everywhere too? *Mourir pour la Patrie*?" She could tell her French words had not delivered the punch she had hoped they would. "Die for the motherland?" Without a beat she began to sing Canada's national anthem in French. Her full-throated rendition made Peter uneasy, as he grasped how drunk she was. He tried to edge his way past her towards the hallway. "Going anywhere?"

"I just thought—I mean, if Jean-Louis's not here, I should probably be going." He was in the hallway, uncertain of just about everything, when he heard Mrs. Lalande call out to him.

"You want to freeze your ass out there?" Agnes knew she was stuck with the boy.

Peter fetched his backpack that he had dropped by the front door and made his way back into the kitchen; he stood there, bag cradled on his toes.

"Do your parents—"

"Don't worry about my parents."

* * *

Jeanine Mercier was endeavoring to put one foot in front of the other, trying not to think about anything else but the task at hand, which, for now, was making ham sandwiches on rye. She layered butter and mustard in equal amounts with slices of ham and some Swiss cheese, placed the top slice of bread, and cut each sandwich in diagonals. She made eight in all, hoping beyond hope that a couple of them might find their way to Peter. She stacked the four baggies into a lunchbox they only used when the family went on vacation—a square tin decorated with the Union Jack her mother-in-law had brought with her from England. This, she told herself, was certainly not a vacation, adding cookies, a May West cupcake, two apples, and three cans of ginger ale into the cooler alongside the lunchbox. Packing beer was out of the question.

When she entered their bedroom, Jeanine found Bob cleaning his shotgun. The weapon was never more threatening, under the circumstances. "Your food's by the back door." She watched as he placed the gun in a soft case, verifying his ammo was in the side pocket. "You sure you want to have that with you?"

Bob lay the weapon on the bed. "I don't know what I'm gonna find out there." He presumed having his firearm was foolish but, given the state of affairs, going into the province of Quebec unarmed seemed even more ill-advised. "I haven't been hunting all these years for no reason," he replied to his wife. His justification for possibly breaking the law was taken at face value.

Jeanine sat on the bed, sliding the gun case away from her. "Bob, I know we haven't done this in a long time."

Bob sat beside her, surprised. "It's not been *that* long!"

Jeanine started laughing like a schoolgirl. She slapped his thigh. "Not that!" She stood up, unnerved by everything. The gun. Her missing teenager. The FLQ ruining the country. All presaged misfortune. "Bob, I'm scared. Come on; let's pray together."

Her husband's look of amazement reminded Jeanine that these were, indeed, extraordinary times. Bob took her hands. She sat back down again, their heads against each other, the moment carried by the tranquility around them.

They had managed a Hail Mary and one Our Father when passion took over. Bob sensed the urge coming from Jeanine, like they had never made love before—this urgency, as though virgins putting the mechanics of sex together for the first time. Jeanine pulled at his belt as Bob kicked off his shoes and lifted her sweater above her shoulders. They embraced, their kisses tearing at each other's lips, and fornicated—two parents who had already suffered a kind of defeat. Leaving for Montreal was postponed till the calm of the next morning.

Thursday,
October 15, 1970

Mrs. Lalande's carpet had lost the stench of vomit that had lingered well into the early hours. The telltale sign of the drunken spillage remained a darkened blotch, even though it had been scrubbed and mopped. Peter was at the toaster, waiting for his bread slices to pop up, when Mrs. Lalande walked in. He could see she had made an attempt at grooming herself. The disheveled hair from the previous evening had been brushed and coiffed with bobby pins, if only half successfully, once Peter got a closer look.

"You're up early."

Peter buttered his toast and sat down at the table. "I feel like I have to get going."

Mrs. Lalande wanted bourbon but decided to try coffee first, considering her company. "Where to?" she asked, pouring herself coffee that Peter had made. She tasted the brew, which was weaker than she preferred.

"I don't know. I thought maybe you might give me some leads." As he said it, given last night's revelations, Peter recognized his request might not be so straightforward.

His hostess walked around him and sat to his right so some of the sunlight would fall against her shoulders. The modicum of warmth soothed her arthritis. "You did?" As with most of her choices, Agnes required trust, and she did not know this young man in the least. She reached for the bottle of bourbon left on the table, for life was too complicated when sober. She added the booze to her coffee mug and imbibed heartily. The combination was especially delicious on an empty stomach. All that was missing, she thought, was a dollop of whipped cream, which she did not have. "How well do you know my Jean-Louis?"

Peter's eyes lit up, like he had a trump card to play here. A veritable twinkle came from him as he replied, "I know stuff about him that you don't."

"You do?" The quinquagenarian liked the cat-and-mouse game Peter seemed to present her with. "And what might that be?"

Only then did it dawn on Peter that he might be betraying Jean-Louis if he disclosed what he had been told in confidence. An uncomfortable sweat appeared on his brow. "It's, umm, a secret," was all he could mutter before swallowing the last of his toast and going to the stove to pour himself a refill.

Agnes knew she had him between a rock and a hard place. Reveal the information, and that made him a traitor to her son. Not revealing it left him without his pivotal request for an address. She felt bad for him but played along anyway. "Secrets? Umm ... from his own mother?" She leaned over the table and held his chin firmly in her hand, treating him like he might have been her prisoner instead of her guest. *Tu penses que t'é le premier p'tit garçon qui frappe à ma porte pour mon fils?*"

Peter took a few seconds to process the French, translating it in his head as best he could. He pulled away from her, hurt by her comment that he wasn't the first boy to knock on her door for Jean-Louis. He was positive that's what she had said; at the very least, implied with the innuendo. Peter endeavored to defend himself. "I'm not interested in him that way, if that's what you mean." Why he had stated his position like that, he wasn't at all certain.

Agnes smiled, amused by the innocence of love she saw all over his face. "Then he must be losing his touch. In his old age." She swigged her coffee and bourbon. "*Écoute.* I don't care who my son sleeps with, okay? But I do care who he kills."

Peter could not fathom her words. What was he meant to make of that?

Before he could comment, Mrs. Lalande crossed over to the counter to a canister with the word *sucre* stenciled on its side. She pulled out twenty-dollar bills. She took a pen and two pieces of paper from a drawer and jotted down some sentences. She handed the money and the folded message to Peter. "Here. Take a cab. If he's not at this address," she said, giving him the separate sheet, "someone there should be able to help you get to him. My note explains who you are—more or less."

Peter tucked the note, together with the cash, into his front jeans pocket for safekeeping. He read the address as though it might be familiar before putting it in his shirt pocket. He took his dirty dishes and rinsed them in the sink. "Did you teach Jean-Louis his English?"

"Why do you ask that?"

"Your English. It's really good. Much better than his—"

"What? We can't speak English in Quebec?"

Peter grasped that his question had been misinterpreted, which made him think of his father. *His* father would have asked that question with exactly that kind of ignorance behind the intent. "No, no, not at all like that," he said in his defense. "Really. I just was ... I mean, I'm really impressed how well you speak. You have no accent."

Agnes Lalande, née Pommier, had had no English in her life until Mr. Pommier was dead and gone, before she turned four. The tedious succession of her mother's lovers, all Anglos, had improved her English-language skills, even while berating or belittling her, until the last two suitors had taken her against her will.

The damage done by Douglas, the policeman, had left Agnes numb. What was another prick up her body, Agnes thought, when she gave in to Dennis rather than struggle? The fight in her had mostly been extinguished by then. A month later, she vacated her mother's apartment and severed all ties—thirty days of gathering belongings for a life she did not want to live. When Agnes shut that door, her mother was as dead to her as her father, whom she could not recollect, not even in the abstract.

No accent! She saw the sick irony in that.

Peter's backhanded compliment brought this rush of pain and suffering for her, along with the remembrance of meeting Lionel at the cusp of her thirties. This sole kernel of joy had changed the trajectory of her directionless life. It was this kindred element about Peter, come into her son's life, that she liked. If Lionel and the cause for an independent

Quebec had turned her existence around, like no other could have, was Peter that for her son?

In her usual dismissive way, Agnes informed Peter that Saint Lambert had a proud English history, going back decades, explaining her facility with English quite cleverly. She escorted Peter down the hallway, half confident that his fortitude would prevail. He bundled up, waiting for the cab to arrive. They saw the taxi pull up front.

"Peter." She took hold of his hand. "Jean-Louis's only tough on the outside. He's got a noble heart. Got it from his dad."

Peter was about to shut the door when he thought of asking her, "Where's ... his dad?"

"He's with him. They're always together."

*   *   *

Jean-Louis was sound asleep on the sofa when the unanticipated knock came at the door. He jumped up like a cat sprung upon by a lurking dog. He reached for the gun from under the seat cushion and proceeded to the door. His unwashed hair was disheveled, and a bright-red crease from the pillow's corduroy border marked his left cheek. Jean-Louis inched quietly in his stockinged feet and peered through the peephole. He grinned, not believing his good fortune. He secured the gun under his belt behind his back before unlocking the door. "*Mon Dieu. De la grande visite.*"

Peter understood those words. It's what his mother said when a relative dropped by unexpectedly. He took a step inside the sparsely furnished space, unable to mask his delight at having located his sought-out prospect. The two stood awkwardly before Jean-Louis pulled Peter further inside. He closed and double-locked the door, then turned to face the boy. There was another pregnant pause before Jean-Louis grabbed Peter into a bear hug. "What a pleasant surprise."

Peter reciprocated, clasping Jean-Louis's back with his arms. No hug had ever felt quite like this one. His fingers pressed and lingered, all experimentation against the muscular leanness under the cotton shirt, until he accidentally knocked the firearm from Jean-Louis's belt. The weapon fell with a thud to the wooden floor, causing them to separate instantly. Both men's eyes were glued—Peter's to the gun; Jean-Louis's to Peter, trying to assess how best to explain.

"Is that a real—"

Jean-Louis was swift. He picked up the Colt pistol and thought of where to safely hide it. He walked to the sofa and returned the firearm to where he had it stowed originally. He sat down and tapped the cushion beside him, hoping the incident with the gun had not ruined the mood.

Peter recalled how Marilyn had tried to sway him when they were on acid in Denise's basement. How different the world seemed now, as Peter chose not to waver.

"Take off your coat. It's hot in here." Jean-Louis sprang to his feet and helped Peter with his gear. "Here. Let me get your backpack." He tossed it towards the hallway that led to the bathroom and bedroom. "Are you hungry? I could use some eggs."

*

Jean-Louis was stuffing himself with scrambled eggs and toast. He sipped from his cup of tea. When he combed his fingers through his hair, he was reminded of how grimy he was. "You look older than I remembered you."

Peter tried to recall if the Jean-Louis from that night was any different than the one before him now. Their twenty minutes of riding together on a bus was a far-distant memory. Peter could hardly breathe when he took it all in, that the handsome man with the hair and eyes that so appealed to him back then was the very same one standing in his stockinged feet before him. "I do?" was all he could muster.

"You do." Jean-Louis snapped his fingers, recollecting his gift of the frog blotters. "You did that acid, didn't you? That's what it is," he said with another snap. "Acid can do that to you."

"You look older too," he retorted, for no other reason than not wanting to be outdone.

"I do? Must be the acid." He said it glibly, not sure of Peter's intent.

"I don't know ..." Peter was frazzled, aware that he was in uncharted territory, feeling an odd need to impress. Not be the naïve boy from Jamesville, searching for a prize he didn't know he wanted. "You don't want to know how I got here?" His question served as temporary decoy.

Jean-Louis left his chair and threw his dishes in the sink. "Oh, I can figure that one out pretty easy." When he turned, he had a mischievous smile for Peter.

"Or why I'm here?"

"For more acid?" he teased.

Peter rose to look out the kitchen window. The snow had begun to fall again, which made him wonder how his parents were faring, if they were worried sick as to his whereabouts in this weather. He knew he owed them an explanation. At the very least, a phone call. He glanced around to see if there was a phone in the room and caught sight of Jean-Louis in his faded jeans, frayed white T-shirt, and thick woolen socks. Peter's insides melted at once; he was at a total loss for words. "That acid got me into a lot of trouble," he said. As if he regretted any of it!

"Acid can do that too." He took a step forward. "It always leaves doors wide open. It's messy like that. No manners at all." He inched nearer to the teen.

"It's okay. I'm okay with it." Peter moved in his direction.

"Do your parents know you're here?"

Peter stopped advancing. "They don't have your mother's address, if that's what you're wondering."

"You're positive about that?" They exchanged communicative nods. They were only a few feet away from each other now. "You're not afraid?"

"Afraid?" Peter asked, conceding, in a way, how out of his depth he was upon hearing that question posed to him.

Jean-Louis bent in to kiss him. Peter's never having kissed a man made his task appear more intricate than it actually was, and he pulled back. Jean-Louis did an exaggerated gesture with his face, his eyes, struck by either Peter's courage or his stupidity. "What? You've never kissed a guy with a gun before?" He set his lips lightly on Peter's cheek.

"It's not the gun that scares me." Peter hesitated

before he countered and kissed the twenty-one-year-old tenderly, wetting their lips.

"Can I make love to you?" Jean-Louis murmured in his ear. "I want to keep you warm," he added, his hand holding Peter's as he shepherded him towards the bedroom.

*　*　*

The falling snow made the house numbers on Chestnut Street harder to decipher from the road. Bob drove his car past a row of apartment buildings interspersed with brick bungalows. At the end of the block, the street was barricaded by a guide-rail to prevent through-traffic. Bob parked the car. Ryan's information was not much to work from, but he gathered up his nerve and walked up to a house with the number 104 beside the mailbox. He rang the doorbell and waited. A young man dressed in loose sweat pants and a sweater answered the door. "*Oui?*"

"I'm sorry to bother you. I'm looking for my son."

"*Quoi?*" The man appraised him as if he were cattle. "*J'm'excuse, mais on parle pas l'anglais icitte.*" With that, he slammed the door.

"Son of a bitch!" Incensed by the rudeness, Bob hurried down the snow-covered path to the next house at 106 Chestnut Street. "I can't believe these people."

The woman at 106, in curlers and a housecoat, had nothing for him. She smiled politely and stood there as Bob retreated. Conscious that she was watching him, Bob reached the sidewalk and went to the curb, hoping for better luck on the other side of the street. He turned and waved back at the woman as she finally shut her door. He was on the front stoop of the apartments at 109, ringing the doorbell, when three unmarked cars drove up the street.

Bob's concentration was on how to pronounce certain French words, oblivious that six officers had swarmed the front lawn right behind him. He was about to say *bonjour* to whomever opened the door when the officers pushed their way through, sweeping him into the living room, confronting Mrs. Lalande as they barged in. "Hey, what's going on here?"

* * *

The hissing from the steam radiator accentuated the bareness of the bedroom. The random clanking from the cast-iron fixture under the window was a reminder of how ancient the tenement was. Jean-Louis and Peter lay naked under the sheets on the mattress that covered the floor. "I was right. You'd never ..."

Peter rolled away from his new lover, embarrassed at having lied to him on the bus back in Jamesville. He sat up against the wall and tucked one of the two pillows in the small of his back for support. "Never. This was it."

"Did you like it?"

Peter jumped on top of Jean-Louis and kissed him passionately as his answer. They rolled about on the mattress, like wrestling teenagers, and began to reengage.

*

"I can't believe we're doing this." Jean-Louis's woolen muffler hid the bottom of his face. Peter ran ahead of him on the path, enjoying their daring. The snow-covered ground made the graves seem Dickensian. The Mont Royal graveyard on this Thursday in October had all the solemnity of a funeral. The occasional pedestrians walking their dogs, the unexplainable diehard joggers sweating in the cold, contrasted sharply with Peter and Jean-Louis's earnest escapade.

"Can it be that bad out there?" Peter had cajoled back at the apartment. His enthusiasm for a stroll had been too disarming.

Police sirens came and went in the distance, as did the engines of low-flying planes in the skies. Jean-Louis's antennae were on high alert, inspecting the park below the cemetery grounds for anything irregular. The view from their terrain was limitless. "You've never been to Montreal before?"

Peter had been to the city twice with his parents. This visit was not that. "Yeah." He reached Jean-Louis and took him by the waist.

"We can't do that out here." The reaction startled Peter. "It's not because it's gay. It's that ... we can't attract attention. Think—anonymous." He caught the boy's glove and squeezed it. "*Tu comprends*?"

"*Oui*. Yeah, I get it." When Jean-Louis hugged him ardently, unable to contain his own conflicted desires, the coldness of their cheeks acted like a shocking, soothing elixir. "We should get back to the apartment," Peter said, knowing he wanted to kiss and fuck the man on the spot.

*

The mattress on the floor had been jostled to the side, pushed closer to the radiator by the fervent sex play. The loud rat-a-tat-tat from the back door in the kitchen made Jean-Louis pause their copulation. He placed his palm over Peter's mouth, his demeanor deadly serious, as though one word uttered could elicit their downfall. He jumped up from the mattress. Peter watched, then followed, as Jean-Louis went to the living room. He saw him take the gun from under the couch pillows and proceed towards the kitchen.

Peter remained in the alcove between the two rooms, hiding his nakedness, petrified at the drama unfolding before him. Jean-Louis tiptoed to the back door. With no peephole, he inched against the wall and peeked through the window to see who was standing on his third-floor porch. The sight of Claire, waiting all alone, let him breathe temporarily. He rushed to open the door. "*Excuse mon costume,*" he told her, not bothering to hide his dangling genitals.

Claire pinched his bare bum, appreciating the view. "*Vite. Y faut qu' tu t'enfuies.*" The distress in her voice, telling him to run, subsided when she saw Peter standing in his own birthday suit. Her astonishment was enough for Peter to speak up.

"Sorry. Should I go?"

For once, Jean-Louis had no immediate answer. "Uh ..." His gaze went from Peter to Claire.

She came to his rescue. "If you want to stay alive, you'd better go," she said to him in French.

"What's happening?"

Jean-Louis's use of English was jarring. Claire loathed speaking the oppressor's tongue, but now was not the time for polemics. "They're picking up everybody they can make a connection to you-know-who." Her English was accented with a French Canadian lilt.

"Noel?" Jean-Louis's confusion was short-lived as Claire's questioning eyes indicated her concern about Peter in their midst. "He's okay," he assured her, somewhat aware that he couldn't say that conclusively.

She knew time was not on their side today to debate. "Don't you remember who they caught and lost the other day?"

"They won't find me here."

Claire was unconvinced. "But at your mom's. They'll go there. They'll come here soon enough." She realized her mission here had been accomplished. She turned the doorknob to leave.

"*Merci.*" His nakedness made a hug impossible. "You're going south?"

Claire turned to him. "*Oui.* Wanta come?"

Jean-Louis understood that had been her intent from the outset. He looked back at Peter, then shook his head in a silent no to her. She blew him a kiss and went out the door.

As soon as she departed, Jean-Louis ran to the bedroom and opened the closet. He took a canvas bag and tossed in the few items of clothing he had with him. He reached for the boxes of ammunition he kept in a duffel bag on the top shelf. "You know how to load guns?"

The only guns Peter had ever held were his father's hunting rifles. "I suppose so." With that brief answer, Peter jumped on board their train. He observed as his newfound boyfriend took out three other weapons from the back of the closet, ensconced behind some wooden slats, and paid close attention as Jean-Louis showed him how each worked, along with the safety mechanisms.

Moments later, in the shower, the two were masturbating each other to a powerful climax; their passion's fury inundated by a thousand questions Peter did not know how to ask or even if he was allowed to do so. When the water was shut off and Jean-Louis handed him a musty towel, Peter simply said, "Where are we going after this?"

The militant replied, "Now you're scared?"

"Yeah."

"You should be. But don't worry. I'll make sure you're safe. How's that?"

Jean-Louis took Peter in his arms when he saw genuine qualm on the teenager's face. He hugged him tightly, more tightly than he had ever held anyone else before. The gravity of running away from home was set aside as Jean-Louis began to dry Peter's hair with the towel.

* * *

Bob's patience was being tested like never before. He was reminded of his war days as he sat on a chair in the living room, surrounded by men in uniform walking about. Sergeant Megan, in his gray shirt and dark-blue trousers, his jacket slightly constricted around the belly, had not foreseen this glitch—a civilian from Ontario who was wasting precious time. "Mr. Mercier, now bear with me, okay? You say you've never met the woman who lives here. You just *happened* to come to this house. Today. Of all days. Just now? Is that your position?" He had Bob's wallet and was twiddling his Ontario driver's license between his fingers.

"It's not my position; it's the goddamn truth," he replied, frustrated by all the repetition. Bob's bladder was bursting to be released, but he knew better than to request a bathroom break. "I'm looking for my son. I showed you his picture. You've got it there." He saw the RCMP official glance again at the boy in the photo and put it in his coat pocket. "Hey, that's mine. I need it."

"You'll get it back," he said, though the arrogant tone behind his promise made Bob doubt he ever would. Megan changed tactics. "Maybe I can help you find him. But first, you help me here." He stood up, stepped to the right, then to the left, like a prosecutor might attempt with the aim of influencing a jury. "Now, you say you didn't have a house number; you were just … guessing. Out of all of the hundreds of thousands of addresses here in Montreal?"

Bob felt his blood pressure rising. He wanted to scream out Peter's name and reproach him for everything that was happening to him. He counted to ten under his breath before speaking again. "I told you …" Bob could see the day, the exact hour, when he had confronted Peter with the mysterious letter. Why had he not just thrown the damn letter away, like he had wanted to do in the first place? He had his wife to blame for that. "You can't do that, Bob," Jeanine had advised him. *That wouldn't be right* had been her exact words. If only she could see how wrong her righteousness had been.

Bob tried with Megan again. "My son received this letter. There were drugs in it. He took the damn drugs and then just took off. In the space of two days. I can't help it that you were coming to this particular house at this particular hour. This is a free country, the last time I checked." Peter's words coming out of his own mouth angered Bob more than he could have imagined. He could feel the weight of the world on his shoulders.

Two officers came into the living room from the kitchen, with Mrs. Lalande in cuffs. The taller of the constables held a revolver in a plastic bag. "We found this in the back bedroom. Looks like it used to be the boy's room. She says she hasn't seen her son in months. Doesn't know where he is."

"*C'est mon fusil.*"

"Now, Agnes," said Megan, standing beside her. "What do you need a revolver for? Guns never helped your family before. Isn't that right?" He knew she had perfect command of English and wasn't about to embarrass himself with his poor French pronunciation.

"You never know when the RCMP are gonna walk in and arrest you for being French."

Megan laughed. He had always enjoyed his interactions with Agnes. Her pluck had a firebrand he could admire, even if he hated all of what her politics represented. "It's not the French we have a problem with. Just their whores!"

The crass remark dumbfounded Bob. "Hey, watch your tongue there."

A constable entered the apartment, carrying Bob's lunchbox and the rifle he had concealed under blankets in his trunk. "We found this." He removed the gun from its cloth case.

"Umm." Megan reached for the weapon and ensured it wasn't loaded. "What did you plan to do with your son, Mr. Mercier? Shoot him?" He returned the rifle to the officer. "Bring 'em both down for questioning." The men holding Mrs. Lalande began to follow his orders, but she stopped in front of Megan. He could smell the liquor on her breath. "You're not going to survive long without a drink, are you?" Without any hesitation, Agnes spit in his face. The officers tugged at her arms to drag her off. "I'll remember that when I get to your lovely Jean-Louis," Megan said in a monotone that threatened. He used his handkerchief to wipe off the slaver. "Maybe I'll use a little spit on him too."

In the distance, he heard Mrs. Lalande caution back. "You'll never take my Louis alive; you know that."

He turned to the officer closest to him. "Get him out of here," he demanded, indicating Bob. Sergeant Megan paused at the threshold to the apartment. "Don't have too much fun with the place, boys," he told the remaining officers.

Crashing glass noises came from inside before he was off the stoop.

* * *

Jean-Louis led Peter down the three flights of stairs behind the apartment building. The twenty-something knew they had wasted valuable time; he was at a loss to explain how smitten he was. Sex in the shower had seemed almost necessary, a symbol that they were undertaking the journey together, going forward. With the duffel bag firmly in place over his shoulders, he let Peter walk past him with the canvas bag, once they were in the backyard. "Best not to talk much. Just follow my lead. Try to stay by my side. If I run, you run with me." They set their headgear down over their foreheads, seeking as much anonymity as they could, traveling east on foot down whichever back alleyway was available.

The sky had dimmed noticeably this late in the afternoon. The intermittent snow that fell over the Montreal topography had harsh north-south winds awaiting them at every street crossing. They had gone a few miles through business and residential sectors and were venturing down another alleyway when Jean-Louis glimpsed a determined Peter at his side. *What am I doing with this Anglo boy?* he thought, though nothing could have induced him to send Peter away.

Peter returned an encouraging smile to his accomplice, bracing himself through the biting cold. He checked to see if anyone was around them. With no one there, he held on to the crook of Jean-Louis's elbow, squeezed, and let go as the two trudged onwards.

* * *

The stash house had been chosen wisely by the

cell. The location, rented by a family unrelated to any of them, was, at least on paper, suitably incognito. The hideaway, nestled in a quiet, working-class suburb, lacked furniture and sufficient heating, but at just a mile south of the highway, it made for an easy escape out of the metropolis.

Peter sat on the single bed, trying to keep warm under thin, cheap blankets. The room was empty, except for the bed and the floor lamp, the bulb of which cast a pasty shard of light. The lampshade, with its water-damage markings, smelled of mildew, Peter thought. He could see brighter light coming from under the door and voices traveling from another room. Peter sat up as footsteps approached.

Jean-Louis opened and closed the door speedily, giving the impression of an imperative that whatever was out there could not come inside here. "They arrested Mom today." He pumped a fist against the wall. Not so loud that it would bring one of his crew to investigate but loud enough for Peter to recoil a few inches. He sat on the bed beside Peter. "*Maudits bâtards!*"

Peter got the gist of his phrase—fuckers, by any other name. His freezing body made him heat-seeking, and he cuddled up to Jean-Louis, warming himself while consoling his friend. "I'm really sorry. She was ... nice to me."

Jean-Louis thought that funny and laughed.

"Nice is not the word I'd use for *moman*." He considered his critique of her. "Maybe if she didn't drink all day long."

Peter's head was against the other man's shoulder, cradled where the crook of the neck blended into the pectoral. "Doesn't your dad mind?"

"My dad?"

Peter sensed Jean-Louis's confusion right away. He moved to look at him. "Yeah. Where is he? I've been meaning to ask all day." They had walked nonstop for three hours to reach their destination. All that, while not speaking. Breathing in unison, aware that there was a mission at hand, with Peter not fully appreciating what that duty was. He was in his own adolescent mystery, only partly of his making. Most of the time—to keep from thinking of how cold and hungry he was—Peter had fantasized his role in the developing drama, casting himself as a teenage lover, which he was. But the task was not so simple when allocating for Jean-Louis. This complicated enigma was not explained as easily. One minute, he had seen his sex partner as a renegade, then a misunderstood brigand on the verge of a grand scheme. The scenarios were as endless as they were incomplete.

Jean-Louis appeared stunned. "Why?"

"Your mom—she said he was with you."

"Here? With me?" Peter's nod made Jean-Louis

sad, an emotion that made him disinclined to answer any more of Peter's questions.

"Is that who's out there in the other room? You didn't want him to meet me. I can keep secrets too, you know." The broken trust he had nearly committed in Mrs. Lalande's kitchen came back to haunt him. Peter blushed.

The boy's response bothered Jean-Louis almost as much as his questions. The discomfort caused Jean-Louis to get up. He went to the window that was masked by heavy curtains and peered outside from the corner of the panes. The amount of snow was minimal, a dusting that accented shadows. "There's something so French Canadian about snow. When I think of who I am, I think of snow. I hope I die in the winter. Seems to make sense, that. Dying in winter."

The swerve in topics made Peter get up as well. He approached Jean-Louis and cradled himself into his arms.

"It's not me you want," Jean-Louis said, pretending to push him away. "You just want my body heat. I can tell."

"You damn right," said Peter, giggling. "My nuts are frozen."

"They are?" He reached inside Peter's pants.

"Ow." Peter winced. "Your hands are like icicles!"

Jean-Louis shifted their bodies sideways to the bed. "We can warm each other up—if you like." He dropped them onto the cramped single bed like they were one giant wrapped sausage.

Their cuddling switched to a tight fetal-ball position, an enmeshment quite complete. "Can we leave here?"

Peter's question had a ping-pong effect, unsettling Jean-Louis. Second thoughts were growing incrementally for both of them, it seemed. "It's not very safe," he said, rubbing the young man's belly. "Maybe you, though. Maybe you can. Why?"

Without any more of a reason than wanting to order pizza, Peter changed the subject. "What's going to happen to your mom?" He heard Jean-Louis's long, pensive sigh; could feel its hotness against the nape of his neck.

"It's crazy out there. Trudeau's gonna do something big. I can just tell. He thinks he's playing cops and robbers. He'll see."

The insinuation had little significance for Peter. All his points of reference to cops and robbers had cowboys and Indians with them, rummaged from television and the movies. He had no more attachment to terrorism than he had to language and culture. His blank slate allowed him to ask, "Like what?"

Jean-Louis let go of him and lay on his back, as Peter remained facing away from him on his side. "You sure you don't want to go home?" he offered the boy, cracking the façade in their armor.

The absurdity of that possibility made Peter move straightaway. He kissed Jean-Louis, making a point of grabbing at the other man's crotch.

"For a guy who's never kissed another guy—" Jean-Louis started to say, but Peter dropped his full weight down onto his body.

"I never want to go home. You're my new home. Wherever you want it to be." Instinctively, Peter slid down to the man's belt and began to undo the buckle. His focus was primal, missing altogether the elusive melancholy as Jean-Louis contemplated the shabby room they were now calling home.

Friday,
October 16, 1970

The lights turned on at an ungodly hour in the provincial jail. Bob stood at the communal toilet, taking a leak, creeped out by the lack of privacy. His three other cellmates had already used the can, one after the other, before Bob dared take his turn. He could feel all eyes were on him while he urinated.

Convict number one, a Jérôme, as far as Bob could recall from the previous night, swung down from one of the top bunks. "So why are you here?" he demanded, his halitosis carving up Bob's nostrils. "And this time, the fucking truth. None of this"—he mimicked an effeminate cadence—"I can't find my son." His contempt for Bob was written all over his furled lip as he turned to his fellow inmates. "The whole fucking country's going up in arms, and this sucker's running around Montreal, searching for his brat of a boy."

Bob flicked off the drops of urine from his penis and zipped up his pants. He wiped his hand on the side of the polyester blend, thinking he could ignore the comment.

The second convict, whose name escaped Bob, got in his face. "Why do I think he just wants a boy to suck him off?" He stabbed a finger into Bob's chest. "Ain't that right, buster? You just like sucking boy cock. That's what got you in here." The man gripped his own crotch and used his tongue to imply fellatio, pretending he was getting some.

Bob pushed the man away, thinking he was demarcating simple territory for himself.

The man thrust Bob backwards, just enough to let him know he was on the losing side of things. "You try that one more time, I swear to you, I'll shove this fist down—"

Bob swerved, ready to punch him, when Jérôme intervened. His huge torso had the strength of two Bobs. He glared down at Mercier. "There's three of us. Unless you want to get fucked real bad, you'd better shut the fuck up. Learn your place." Jérôme could tell this fish was in for a hell of a beating. "You're in the slammer with the rest of us. You're a prisoner now. Like it or not. You been checked." He placed his knuckles on Bob's chin, leaving little unsaid.

A couple of burly guards arrived at their door. The fattest one made a sign to someone down the hall, and the automatic metal door slid open. Four more prisoners were tossed inside.

"What the fuck's going on here?" Jérôme asked, moving towards the guards for an explanation.

A baton placed in front of Jérôme stopped him cold. "Get used to it. The War Measures Act was declared this morning around dawn."

"*C'est quoi çà?*"

Bob heard the second convict ask the others what that meant. He had an inkling that the Act took away their rights, but he was not about to educate his aggressors. The eight men, crammed together, tried to shuffle around, hoping to make the best of a nasty situation. A gentleman dressed in a three-piece custom-tailored suit put out his hand. Bob shook it willingly.

* * *

Dawn was held at bay by the heavy drapes in the stash-house bedroom. Peter and Jean-Louis were fully dressed, wearing their jackets under the skimpy blankets. The twin-sized bed had made their night's sleep tight and romantic. There was a knock at the door before a male voice announced that there was fresh coffee. Jean-Louis got up. When he returned, he carried an oversized mug and a plate of food. "It's not the Ritz, but …"

Peter sipped from the communal cup. He tasted a piece of hard cheese, liked it, and made himself a sandwich with the slices of bread. Jean-Louis went to the window and parted the drapes an inch. The eastern horizon had a gorgeous glow, a slit of light with orange-red on its arc. He carefully replaced the thick material so that nothing from inside could be seen from the outside. He turned to Peter, who was eating quietly. "We have an errand for you."

*

The Montreal streets had an eerier stillness than Peter remembered from a few days before. Or was his heightened sense of obligation, tasking his nerves, making him susceptible to a more vivid imagination? He could not say. He reached the Metro entrance and walked down the stairs. Everyone on the train had an air of uneasiness, circumspect to the point of paranoia, Peter thought; he was convinced that he stood out as a total outsider in their midst. He held on to the leather briefcase he had been given, hoping and praying he would not mess up his instructions.

At the bank, he presented himself to the service desk and did exactly as Jean-Louis had told him to do. The shirt and tie he had been furnished, his hair combed and pomaded, did make him appear more mature, and with that makeover came some needed confidence. After presenting the administrator with his fake ID, the man escorted him to a secure room. Each took their turn with their separate keys at the metal wall, slotted, floor to ceiling, with safe-deposit boxes, before the employee left him with the slim steel container. Inside the box, Peter found the passports, along with two envelopes. He placed the items faithfully inside a zipped pouch in the interior of the briefcase.

Out on the street again, he checked the piece of paper for his next address. The sun's brilliance made the day's tasks more pleasurable. The heat on his skin was almost magical, even under the circumstances. Twenty minutes later, standing kitty-corner from the store, Peter glanced around for any fishy activity. He had been warned to be on the lookout for undercover officers, so he bent down to tie his boots, then lit a cigarette, pretending he was waiting for someone. When he thought the coast was clear, he advanced and entered the variety store.

The space was poorly lit, with shelves stocked meagerly, which suggested bad management or shortages. At the counter, he uttered the phrase he had been taught to memorize. "*Nous vivons tous dans l'ombre maintenant*," he said in his contrived French. Peter understood what he had said—we all live in shadows now—but was vague on how this communication would translate into action. If the woman was surprised by his presence or his accent, it was not apparent to him.

Peter detected the ammonia of cat urine as soon as she guided him to a back room that was even gloomier than the store. When she put out her palm, he gave her the passports and the envelopes. In exchange, she produced a thicker envelope that was hidden behind an old, ratty painting of some pope he only half recognized. Peter dropped the item into his case.

Without a word, she led him to a door and put a finger over her mouth, indicating that silence was essential upon exiting. "*Un instant*," she whispered to him.

Hearing her speak felt odd to Peter, as though some conspirator code had been breached. He watched as she went to the front. He could hear her bustling. When she returned, she had a bag filled with groceries. The shopkeeper presented him the parcel and opened the back door. Without even looking first, she ushered him out of her establishment. Peter had taken a step forward into the back alleyway when a bulky orange tomcat slipped by his feet and into the backroom, meowing that he did not belong out there a moment longer. The door closing behind Peter reminded him that his assignment was far from over.

Once outside, he had to reorient his bearings. He walked in the opposite direction down the alleyway to get to the busy thoroughfare listed on his instructions. As planned, he tore up the paper with all the notes written for him and ditched the scraps into a nearby garbage can.

He was by the bus stop when the phone booth caught his attention. Without even thinking, he filed into it and closed the folding door. He counted his coins and dialed Ryan's number. Peter couldn't believe his luck when Ryan answered. "What are you doing home?"

"Fuck—where the fuck are you?" Ryan asked, full of animation.

Hearing his friend's voice made all the difference in the world. Where before Peter had been an outlier, free-falling, unable to quite gauge how he felt about any of his endeavors these last few days, now Peter suddenly experienced a grounding effect, earthly and tactile. "I only have a minute," he said, unsure of how much long-distance his quarters and dimes had bought him on the pay phone.

"Dude, you have to come back. It's really crazy here. Did your dad find you?"

"My dad? What are you talking about?"

Ryan had hardly elaborated on the story, mentioning the War Measures Act in passing, when the minutes ran out on the call. Peter heard Ryan plead for him to come home, but the line was disconnected before Peter could make sense of it all.

"Fuck," Peter exclaimed, pounding the metal shelf with his clenched fist. "Fuck," he repeated, struggling to decide if he should call back, but the city bus, careening from nowhere, made him run to catch it instead.

The return bus trip was protracted compared to his Metro ride to midtown, his incessant need to pee stretching out the pace torturously. When Peter got off the bus from the back exit, he resumed his vigilant stance. He had reached the block where the stash house was located when he became aware of a dark sedan driving down the street. The man at the wheel had an aura of surveillance that could not be discounted. Peter continued past the house. He went around the corner and ducked down the alleyway so he could be positive he was not being watched. He hid behind a garbage dumpster and took the time to relieve himself, creating an alibi, should he be detained for questioning. When he stepped out from behind the metal bin, he went along to the next block and repeated his tracks. With no sedans in sight, he assumed it was safe to knock on the front door.

Jean-Louis let him into the vestibule. They could hear Trudeau from the television in the living room. Peter stopped in his tracks, wanting to hear the bulletin. "To bow to the pressure of these kidnappers, who demand that the prisoners be released, would be not only an abdication of responsibility, it would lead to an increase in terrorist activities in Quebec."

Jean-Louis tried to nudge Peter towards the bedroom, adamant that the identity of the other occupants be kept secret, but Peter resisted, standing his ground, wanting to know what was happening.

The usually jocular Trudeau remained monotone and deliberate. "At the moment the FLQ is holding hostage two men in the Montreal area. They are threatened with murder. During the last twelve days, the governments of Canada and Quebec have been engaged in constant consultations. If a democratic society is to continue to exist, it must be able to root out the cancer of an armed revolutionary movement that is bent on destroying the very basis of its freedom."

Jean-Louis, wary that he had crossed too many lines already, forced Peter to go with him to the bedroom, ignoring the three men in the smoke-filled living room. He took the bag of groceries and the briefcase and left hastily. When he reopened the door, he tossed an apple to Peter and peeled the banana he had brought for himself.

"I don't know why I can't see anybody. I mean, if I'm gonna get killed with all of you, I might as well know who I'm giving up my life for."

"Killed?" Jean-Louis proceeded towards the bed and sat beside Peter. "Who said anything about getting killed?"

"You haven't been out there today. It's like living in the States. Like those pictures you see of Vietnam on the news every night. It isn't Canada anymore."

Hearing Peter say that reminded Jean-Louis of how little he understood of their cause. Enthralled as he was with Peter's devotion—undertaking the errands he had run for them at a high risk to his safety—he had to speak up. "This isn't Canada. This is Quebec," Jean-Louis said, knowing he sounded miffed. "That's the whole point of our fight!"

Peter rose from the bed to toss his apple core but realized there was no garbage can. He held on to the core. "Jean-Louis, there's armored tanks and soldiers everywhere." Was that what they were fighting for? An occupied Quebec?

"We didn't put 'em there. *C'é pas d' notre faute.*" Jean-Louis paused, not wanting to bicker. "Were you followed?" He had a nagging suspicion. "Did anyone ..."

Peter hesitated, unsure if his hunch about the sedan had even been valid. "Don't worry." He remembered the Kleenex in his pocket and took it out to wrap the remains of his apple. He thought of placing it on the window sill but gave it to Jean-Louis to dispose of. "I managed to lose them."

"You were *followed*?" Before Peter could expound on his interpretation of events, Jean-Louis moved to the door and ran out. Peter could hear him yell in French to the others—that they had to leave fast, he thought he heard him say. He exited into the hallway, only to be pushed back inside by Jean-Louis. The action had been a reaction, all drawn on adrenaline, but it came off as violent, upturning their rapport.

Peter pulled away angrily. "You're not my parent!"

Jean-Louis instantly altered his posture. "I'm sorry. *Vraiment, j'm'excuse*." He knew not to try and advance any closer to Peter. "It's for your own good. It's safer this way."

"Is that what your father told you to do?"

"My father? Is that what you—" Again, Jean-Louis vacillated, aware of this improbable impasse. "Yeah, you're right. That's what my father taught me. Save your neck. At all costs. And take your secrets with you to the grave."

"I'd like to meet your father. He sounds like an interesting guy." He took a step towards Jean-Louis, wanting to appease. "Who else is out there with him? I thought I heard a woman speak. Is that the same woman—"

The knock on the door interrupted him. "*On est prêt. Tu t'en viens*?" Peter did not recognize Noel's voice. Only the hurried message to leave with them registered.

"*Allez-vous-en*," Jean-Louis replied. "*J'v'a prendre la direction ouest*."

Peter studied Jean-Louis for signs of imminent abandonment. He heard Noel say something about him but couldn't quite catch the phrasing. Had he ordered Jean-Louis to dump him, leave him here to fend for himself?

Peter could hear footsteps and a door opening in the distance, followed by a car driving out of the driveway. Their departure left the premises with an obscure emptiness. Peter sensed the change was all about them. He blamed himself but only partly. He had undertaken what was asked of him, and for that, he was unabashedly proud. "You didn't want to go with your dad?"

Jean-Louis smiled, almost benevolently. He reached for his pack of cigarettes and lit one. He offered it to Peter, who accepted. They smoked quietly, sharing the cigarette back and forth in a hybrid meditation.

"How is it between you and your dad?"

"Peter, my dad's dead."

"What do you mean?" Peter had the cigarette and handed it to Jean-Louis. He went to the bed and sat down, questions swirling in his head. "When? Your mom said—"

"My mother's full of scotch. She was—"

As though coming out of a daydream, for the first

time in days, Peter announced, "My dad's at your mom's house, I think."

The FLQ combatant stopped smoking. "What? How? You told me—" He ran to the window and glimpsed outside. He spotted two men sitting in a dark sedan. "*Fuck. Ostie d'câlisse!*"

"What is it?"

"I hope you know how to shoot."

Peter darted to the other side of the window. The vehicle was the same sedan as before. "I wasn't followed here. I swear to you."

Jean-Louis wasn't listening. "How do you know? How can I believe you? You told me—"

"I called a friend while I was out. That's how I know about Dad."

"You *called* someone!" Jean-Louis's incredulity was not lost on Peter. "Are you crazy? Fuck!"

"It's not what you think." How could he explain himself without coming off as reckless? "I just wanted to let him know I was okay. He said my dad came over to his house. He pressured him to give up the address you put on the envelope."

"*Maudite marde!*"

"I'm sorry," was all Peter could marshal; his call to Ryan an impulse that, in retrospect, had been cavalier.

"It's easy to be sorry when you're dead." Jean-Louis ran out of the room again, with Peter on his heels. In the bedroom next to theirs, Jean-Louis prepared the rifle and the revolver that Peter recognized from the apartment. The novice took the revolver and practiced aiming it. "*Fais attention*. Be careful."

"Why can't we just leave like the others?"

"The others are probably being escorted to jail by now. I'm *never* going to jail."

Peter's adrenaline spiked. The pronouncement sounded so fixed, not at all arbitrary. "Maybe they got away. How do you know? *I* got away. I know nobody followed me here." He said it with such conviction, conscious that he had no proof of that. "I made sure of that," he added, wanting to pacify the building tension between them. "Anyway, they don't know who I am, right? I could leave." The proposition was out before Peter realized he hadn't meant it quite like that. He wanted to stay. He did not want to leave Jean-Louis's side.

The man took the rifle and went to the living room, asking as he walked off, "Is that what you want?"

Peter didn't answer right away. He grasped that what he had to say might not matter anymore. He slipped to the opposite side of the window and peered out. The street was empty. "They're gone."

Jean-Louis could see as well that the car had driven off. He went to their bedroom and came back with the pack of cigarettes and lit one. The nicotine flushed through his system, settling his rattled nerves. "It's up to you. It could be some kind of ambush.

They're not stupid, you know." But he could not evade a feeling of responsibility for Peter's safety. "What do you want to do?"

Peter tried to envision his options. He was torn between what he knew and what he didn't know. Jamesville, for him, was light-years away now, no more than a dog-eared version of himself that he didn't want. Of that, he was quite certain. "If my dad's looking for me ... maybe he's at your mom's. Around there. My friend didn't have your exact address."

Jean-Louis avoided his gaze. The activist in him recognized that Peter did not belong with him. He had not journeyed the obligatory path to get here. He was merely a seventeen-year-old boy caught up in a love affair that had transposed lust for love, but when he looked up and saw the blue of Peter's irises, the clarity in them frightened Jean-Louis. Was Peter willing to die for him in the same way he was willing to die for the cause? That yoke weighed too heavily on him, fearing he had been the source of that creation. Peter approached, presenting him the revolver. "You don't want to keep it?" Jean-Louis asked him. "Just in case?"

Peter had considered all the possibilities of how that could go wrong and gave him the weapon. He put out his hand in a gesture of friendship, wavering over how leaving was done in situations like these.

Jean-Louis took it. *Gentlemen in a business deal*, he thought.

"How ... did he die?" Peter appeared sullen, like he had known the man. "Your dad?"

"We don't know. It was ages ago. Police custody. Good old RCMP. We never did get any real answer. A cover-up. Autopsy notes disappeared. You know how it is when you're a fanatic French. *On compte pas pour beaucoup*."

Peter was sure he disagreed with that. He wanted to say, "Of course everyone counts," but he kept that opinion to himself. He took a moment before inquiring, "Was it for a noble ... cause?"

"*La Patrie*." Jean-Louis couldn't tell if Peter knew the meaning of the word. "Always a noble cause, the homeland, right? He planted ... a bomb—if that makes any difference to you."

If it did, Peter showed no signs of it. He took his coat from the floor and began to zip up. He knotted his scarf the way his mother had taught him, doubling the width to make the material warmer. He was just playing for time, incapable of fathoming what was about to transpire.

"You should hurry, in case they come back." Jean-Louis had not cried in years, and he was not about to now.

"What about you? What's gonna happen to you?"

"You care?" Jean-Louis asked him, knowing how foolish that was, bringing in sentimentality when that was the last thing needed. Peter's eyes watered as though they might gush any minute. "Go get my bag. It's by the bed," Jean-Louis said, checking out the window to confirm nothing was amiss. He pulled the curtain and, with the butt of his gun, broke a windowpane in case he needed to start shooting. Jean-Louis searched the side pocket of the bag Peter dropped at his feet. He retrieved a two-inch green frog made of glass. "*Tiens*. This is for you."

Peter held the ornament in his palm, admiring the crafted decoration.

"Did you know that the Japanese word for *frog* and for *return* is the same?" Jean-Louis struggled to recall the word but came up blank. "I can't remember the Japanese word, but anyway—it's for a safe return. You'll come back to me. I know it." He pointed to Peter's chest. "*Icitte. Tu t'rappelles-tu, c'que j't'ai dit?* It's in your soul that you're French. Never forget that."

Peter kissed the green frog like one would a lucky charm and tucked it into his inside coat pocket.

Jean-Louis embraced him affectionately. When the passion stirred for both of them, Jean-Louis separated as hastily as he could. "You'd better leave. Now. Before I have to fuck you again." He slapped Peter's bottom hard, as if to say, *if that's the last between us*.

Peter walked towards the back door. Jean-Louis

cocked the rifle and prepared to begin shooting, should they have miscalculated their circumstances.

Outside, in the backyard, Peter attempted to hold back the flood of tears he had not anticipated. This departure had little in common with leaving home, so why was he as bewildered by the set of emotions coming out of him as when he had left his parents' house? Today had seemed endless, from beginning to now; had corroborated this fresh perspective he had of himself. He knew how young he was, but it was as though in one day's measure, he had grown up completely. He reached for the frog, its shape and texture reassuring, and he ran through the yard, jumping over the fence like his life had never mattered as much as it did now.

* * *

Sergeant Megan was at his desk, writing up the release certificate, while Superintendent Higgins stood sentinel in front of him.

The senior official scratched his hoary pate, which concealed dandruff but not his thinning hair. The itchy scalp, a symptom of being at cross purposes with his own instincts, left him mindful of the lame conditions related to Agnes's release. The entire Lalande family gave Higgins pause. "There's no guarantee she'll lead us anywhere." The sergeant continued scribbling, paying no heed to his caution. "You know that, Megan. Right?"

Higgins could not have been more cogent, a quality he had lacked while on supervising duty the night Lionel had died in their custody. A newly minted staff sergeant back then, he had signed off on the warrant for Lionel Lalande's arrest on charges of planting and detonating an explosive device. He could still see Megan, a conceited upstart in his constable uniform, reporting back to him, minutes after the fatality had occurred. Their entanglement in the errant fiasco had sealed their bond, one that Higgins had come to regret. *Stuck again*, he thought, as though they had come full circle without ever getting off their merry-go-round. "She's always been tough, that one." The senior officer skimmed over the certificate ensuring there were no glaring inaccuracies. "You're letting her keep the revolver? No prohibitions?"

Megan had weighed out that dilemma. He wanted her release without prohibitions to keep the playing field skewed in his favor. His shrug made the decision appear pragmatic. He waited for more feedback on his draft. When none was forthcoming, he dialed his subordinate to inform him that the document was ready to process. "Sir"—he took a drag from his cigarette—"she's desperate for a drink. And she still won't budge. If she's on the outside and word gets back to the son—who knows? He might just think it's a safe place to head to." Even as Megan said it, he knew those odds were slim. All reports on the known members of Jean-Louis's cell had stated they had relocated quickly. Moved too fast for anyone to be caught as yet. "I know Noel got away from us, but we'll get them." He was thinking of all the addresses that had not given up any clues. "Someone from inside's tipping them. I'd bet a year's salary on that one."

The superintendent was disinclined to such treachery in their unit. He put out his cigarette stub in the ashtray that was on top of the cluttered bookcase. "She's smarter than you think."

"The men in her life, maybe, but Agnes? Nah. She's harmless. Just a drunk, sir. Worried about last call. She's capable of acting stupid and giving us a lead—anything." Megan was only half persuaded by the potentiality he described and hoped with all his heart that it would play out. He would have liked nothing better than to prove everyone wrong. His unfinished business with the Lalandes went beyond any call of duty.

Higgins gave Agnes more credit than that. "Her heart's with the movement, even if her actions aren't directly connected."

The constable assigned to Megan for his shift knocked and picked up the certificate. Megan took a sip of bitter, cold coffee and spit it back into his cup. "Shit."

"Don't be so sure," Higgins warned him. He was standing at the door. "She still blames us for Lionel." He was being generous in the usage of *us*, he thought, for his role in the conspiracy had been purely bureaucratic. Administrative red tape applied officiously to save the necks of others. That's what he told himself, preferring that to the self-serving means that had saved his own career. His hands had not been dirtied in the death of anyone, criminal or otherwise, to keep him up at night. He was thankful of that much.

The mention of that tally by Higgins made no difference to Megan, whose conscience was intact. The official record had exonerated him and his fellow officers of all misconduct—self-defense, a catchall phrase that tilted the scales of justice mostly in favor of the RCMP. For Megan, that was the only validity that mattered.

* * *

The jail where Agnes had been detained was an impressive structure that reminded her of an octopus with tentacles made of bricks. The wings of the facility stretched out and stretched up with an old-world aura, suggesting a king might have ordained it into existence, rather than being built by a democratically elected body. Agnes had been inside before but never as an inmate. The only areas she had seen were the ones where the visitors were herded on special days. Clean and quiet, if not sterile. She understood more plainly now all the tales she had heard about the jail over the years. There was no exaggeration to the claims. The place was hell on earth.

Her prison stay, brief as it was, had shocked her system to the core. Placed in restrictive custody, unable to communicate with other inmates, had made scoring alcohol impossible. As soon as Agnes could, once outside the gates, her sole mission turned to finding a store that sold liquor. She was sweating profusely, trying to control tremors that made her hands shaky. She placed the bottle of scotch on the market counter, thankful that she had sufficient money in her purse when she'd been hauled off to jail.

She walked dutifully down the street, careful not to attract too much attention as she opened the bottle from the bag and guzzled back. A wave of safety went through her body, no different than if a needle had been introduced into her veins. The toxic blend of pleasure and pain met somewhere halfway betwixt panic and shame. She supported herself against the brick wall, tears welling in her eyes, as she drank half the mickey to steady her nerves. She didn't have a watch, but the darkening skies informed her that she needed to make haste if she wanted to beat the government curfew.

* * *

The same hellhole of a prison had filled up throughout the day as the scope of the War Measures Act expanded exponentially. Shortly after dinner, two officers walked down the landing where Bob's cell was situated, marching a dozen arrestees alongside them. The cell door opened, and a ninth person was added to their numbers. *"C't'assez-là, hein. Viarge!"* Jérôme's ire was lit. *"Eh, c'est ben la dernière fois que j'passe mes vacances icitte."*

Everyone laughed at the vacationing joke, all except for Bob, who had understood little of the sentence.

"Hey, English pea soup, didn't you get it?" The convict addressing Bob had been his nemesis from the start. The only time he had spoken to Bob was to boss him around. That Mathieu detested the English was all Bob knew about the man.

"I got it," Bob said, an air of the wisecracker about him, wishing there was somewhere he could hide. He had adjusted to the comradery that crept in slowly; even Jérôme's crude toughness had grown on him. Only Mathieu was altogether insufferable. The expression of hate that came from him left Bob cold.

Mathieu, mistaking civility for weakness, moved in for his kill. "You did? Well, tell it to me in English. I like an English joke now and then." His thick, unvarnished accent, for some reason, made the dare more tenable.

Bob tried for a seat on a bottom bunk, wanting to get away, but gave up when no one allowed him the courtesy. "I don't need to be teaching any ignorant Frenchman."

"Whoa, whoa, whoa," Jérôme intervened. He was right in Bob's face. "You gotta problem with counting, don't you? There's eight of us now and one stupid fuck like you." He paused for effect. "You don't learn. That's your problem, Monsieur Englishman."

The latest addition to their ranks addressed Bob directly. The man was well into his sixties, attired in a distinguished suit that resembled Richard's, the only inmate who had introduced himself to Bob in a friendly fashion that morning. "What's your name?" He could see Bob hesitating, unsure of what kind of game was afoot. *"C'est quoi son nom encore?"* he asked the others.

"Bob," Mathieu told him.

The educated man, who had no discernable accent when he spoke English, inched towards Bob. "As long as we're in jail together, we might as well be civilized. I'm Eric Loisier." His outstretched hand was rebuffed.

"Civilized? You call bombing and kidnapping civilized?"

Eric considered the question methodically, intrigued by the man he had before him. "You take issue with kidnapping and bombings?"

Bob was convinced this was a setup. For the first time since arriving in the jail cell, he wondered if he would make it out alive. "What do you think?"

"I take issue with being a white nigger in a no-man's-land. Mr. ... uh? Oh yes, you haven't introduced yourself yet."

"Bob Mercier," he said, emphasizing the English pronunciation of the family name.

"Mercer *ou* Mercier? Umm, now, *un instant*." Loisier was instantly fascinated by the paradox before him. "I thought I was speaking to an Englishman. Mercier. *C'est Canadien*? No?"

Bob had heard this tired dogma all his life. "We lost our French years ago. It means nothing to me. Not a damn bit."

Loisier moved back, as though redirecting his cross-examination of a witness. "Very sorry to hear that. Because to me, it means everything."

The round of applause in the cell ricocheted against the walls. The deafening clatter intimidated Bob. "Look at you all. Applauding *what*? It's a goddamn language; that's all. It's no big deal. You can speak all the French you want. You got your schools. Your churches. Why did you have to try and ruin it for the rest of us?"

"*Si on l'tuait. Ça ferait du bien*," Mathieu said, getting a few laughs.

Eric could see Bob was clueless that his life had just been threatened. He raised his arms, intimating to the others, *not now*. He leaned back against the cell door. "Can I ask you a question, Bob?"

Bob was skeptical of any debate within these confines, but Eric, being a salvation of sorts, was too good a chance to pass. He approached him. "Shoot."

"Is Mercier a French name?"

This shibboleth from the language police had been used on Bob so often that he was adept at refuting the trope. "It's not French; it's not English. It's just a goddamn name—that's all. No big deal."

The philosophy professor—for that was Loisier's profession when not inside a jail cell—took in a deep breath, patiently weighing out the pros and cons of his wayward student's hypothesis. "Okay. Would you agree that at one time it came from a French country, say, maybe France?"

Bob nodded reluctantly.

"*Merci*. So, do you—happen to speak any French?"

"Oh, here we go. I know where you're going with this one."

"Humor me. Do you?"

"A bit."

A prisoner who had kept to himself since being incarcerated exclaimed, "*Ah qu' yé menteur*!" Everyone laughed, suspecting this was closer to the truth.

"I got that! I'm not a liar. I used to know some. I just don't practice it anymore. But my wife—she's French."

Loisier seemed pleased by that detail. "Oh, she is? That helps me a lot." Here, Eric paused, hoping his intuition would pan out to be correct. "So, do you have kids, Monsieur Mercier?"

Bob disliked being addressed that way. It reminded him of elementary school with the nastiest of the teachers who made a habit of doing this. "Yes, I have kids. It's my youngest who got me here in the first place. Running off to God knows what, to God knows who, in this damn province of yours."

"And your kids, Mr. Mercer," Loisier continued, balancing between the English and French pronunciation of his surname, "do they speak any French?"

"They do."

"The truth—come on, the truth for once!" he said, in an accusatory fashion that suited a priest more than a professor.

"My kids don't need to speak French. This is

North America. What purpose does it serve, speaking French, when you have the US of A breathing down your throat? English—that's the only language you need. You're all wacky, the whole lot of you."

Bob threw out the indictment, feigning indifference, like he was unaware of the chaos that had brought him to this prison—the National Guardsmen, the RCMP, and the local authorities breaking into houses and apartments, rounding up citizens in all walks of life. His being confined had not broken his trust in the law-and-order functions of government he believed in deeply.

Loisier stepped away from Bob. With what limited space there was, he made his way to the other side of the cell so that he could address them all. "I'm glad I'm in this cell with you today. It helps me to understand my own position better. It helps me to know that I made the right choices along the way. You see, Monsieur Mercier, like it or not, you're part French. You may not belong here, but you're a part of us." Bob tried to interrupt but was silenced with, "*S'il vous plaît!*"

Bob recognized that plea only too well. He could hear Jeanine's voice; imagine her begging him not to screw things up. The youngest of his cellmates stood up from the end of the bed and indicated for him to sit down. Fearing for his safety, Bob acquiesced.

"You may not like that fact. You may detest it for

any of a thousand reasons. And I have no problem with that. For you, that is. For me, I feel it's sad. You have no history. You have no heritage except what you've fashioned. Out of fiction, I might add. You think your kids are Anglos now. But you've stolen from them something that was as simple as an extra language and as rich and complex as a mother tongue. Maybe you've managed to replace it with an ounce or two of English spirit. Notice, I don't call it *soul*. But I doubt it very much, Mr. Mercier. Your problem is that you've lost something that you never knew you had. An identity that went deeper than you'll ever be able to comprehend. You missed the most important baptism."

"Don't bring in religion with me."

"Religion?"

"You said baptism."

"I'm an atheist. The baptism I'm referring to is being soaked in language and culture. Baptism by fire, if you like."

Bob remained stationary.

"You had the option to create from it anything you wanted. Turn it into something unique; make it real. But instead, you opted out, Robert." He pronounced his Christian name, rolling the first R. "You threw it away because you bought into the mind-set of those in power. Well, me, Monsieur

Mercier, I'm proud to be *Canadien*." He made sure that Bob knew he hadn't meant Canadian with an A but with an E by the way he underscored the last syllable. "I'm proud to be able to decimate my language into a dialect that's richer than the cavernous diamond mines of Africa. *Mon joual, y m'appartient. Pis mon bon français aussi, si je le choisis. Pis ma belle province de Québec.*" He didn't expect Bob to understand, so he translated it for his sake. "My slang belongs to me. And my good French, when I want to choose it. And my beautiful province of Quebec." Eric shifted towards Bob, speaking softly for emphasis, so unlike the Mathieus of the world. "But the bastards in Ottawa and Toronto refuse to acknowledge a special right that's tied with my history. *That's* why there's a war out there today. And why I'm ready to fight for it any way I can. I'm proud to be in here."

The thrust of Eric's speech was impossible for Bob to bear. He went to the bars of the cell door, as if propping himself against them would give him more air to breathe. "I just want to get out of here," he said offhandedly.

Eric chose to retire where Bob had been seated. He was also that much nearer to him when he spoke. "For what? Your real jail cell out there?" The ones who understood more English caught the nuance and concurred, smiling in agreement. "You're right about one thing. You really don't belong here, Mister Mercer."

Bob stayed put, looking away from all the men, hoping beyond hope that someone else might join in the fray so that he could be ignored entirely.

*   *   *

Agnes could not escape the cold throughout the apartment. Seated in her favorite recliner, she took a sip of bourbon and set down the glass onto the food tray next to the chair. The thought of raising the thermostat occurred to her, but she tugged at the buttons of her scruffy cardigan instead, too lazy and too comfortable to bother getting up. She picked at the mashed potatoes on the plate beside her and nibbled. Some chicken, a slice of tomato. Her attention went to the television when she saw a clip of people getting arrested. She raised the volume control on the remote.

"No one has an accurate count of those arrested. Three hundred, five hundred," she heard the newsman say as the camera panned to some elderly man being escorted into a police vehicle. Mrs. Lalande smiled when he raised a V-sign of victory before a soldier pushed him away from the camera.

The newsman continued. "No one knows where they'll be taken or how long they will be detained. Since no crime needs to be stated in order for the arrests to take place ..." The anchorman's voice faded as it cut to the War Measures Act speech delivered by the prime minister. Agnes's focus was riveted, primarily out of disgust for what she thought was an overreaction by the federal and provincial governments. She was about to mute it again when the broadcast resumed at the studio news desk. "There are no signs that either of the kidnap victims is any closer to being found."

The doorbell ringing startled Agnes. She got out of the chair as rapidly as she could manage, her legs beleaguered by alcohol. She crept to the window to see who was out there and walked to the front door in haste. "You shouldn't be here. It's not safe." With some reluctance, she let Peter inside, scanning the street to see if anyone was with him, unable to mask her disappointment at his arriving alone.

"I went around the house twice. I didn't see anyone following me. If they're out there, I couldn't see them." He wiped the wet snow off his shoulders.

"You learned fast." Agnes headed back to her chair and her booze. "What brings you here?" She gulped from her tumbler, certain that she needed the reinforcement. "No place to call home?" She gave him a see-I-told-you-so look, and Peter acknowledged grudgingly that she might be right. He slipped off his boots and walked towards the food. "You hungry?" The boy's nod induced some pity for him. "I hardly touched any of it. Help yourself." She gave him the clean spoon and shut off the television but not before Peter caught sight of the footage of people being rounded up. "It's pretty bad out there."

"I know." His reply had substance to it. He swallowed some chicken. "I didn't expect you—here."

Agnes was intrigued. "Oh, and where did you expect me to be?"

Peter shrugged, then added, "I don't know." He returned to his eating.

Agnes leaned to the side and picked up the whiskey bottle to refresh her drink. "If you want to live this kind of life, you have to learn how to lie much better than that." She took another sizeable sip. There was no denying that Peter's presence was more taxing than she was willing to admit. "You thought I'd be in jail! I know how word gets out."

Peter admired this woman, who was quite unlike his mother. He finished the remainder of what was on the plate and licked the spoon.

"How is—" She was too afraid to complete the question. "You want a drink?" Agnes didn't wait for him to answer. She went to the liquor cart she kept in the living room, took two snifters and a decanter of Courvoisier, and poured them each a glass. She handed him his. "It'll steady your nerves."

Peter sampled the alcoholic beverage. His throat burned as the liquid made its way down. He took another sip. "When did you get out?" He could feel his eyes watering and heat coming from his belly.

"A while ago." Mrs. Lalande was back in her seat. Expensive brandy after dinner was not an everyday occurrence, so she relished the taste, trying to appreciate the luxury as much as she could. "They let me out." She said it sarcastically, as if she couldn't figure out why.

Peter recognized her logic and gave her a knowing glance. "He's okay. He's safe."

"For now." Agnes belted back the remainder of her brandy, forgetting altogether her promise to savor it. "Was he happy—to see you?"

Peter smiled sheepishly. He lifted up his glass to indicate his request for a refill.

"Help yourself. But beware. It's got a kick to it."

He poured himself another brandy. "Did a man come searching for me, by any chance?"

"*Ton père*? Yeah. Your dad was here."

Hearing her confirm what Ryan had disclosed to him made Peter put his drink down on the side table. "Where is he?"

She could see he was afraid. "I don't know."

Seeing real fear in the young man reassured her somehow. "He went to jail, like the rest of us."

Peter stood, horrified. "Jail?" He could tell he sounded like a ten-year-old. "My dad? That can't be? Not my dad!"

"Why?" She was insulted by the inference. "He's better than us?" She took the last of her whiskey and emptied the glass. Being without alcohol in her system for twenty-four hours had thrown off her tolerance level. She could feel the room spinning and had to hold back from any movement. She eased her palms against her temples, hoping the dizzying sensation was temporary.

"I have to go. I have to get him." Peter began to leave.

"Hey, are you crazy? There's a curfew out there." She wanted to get up to assert herself but couldn't. "You can't get to the city at this time of night anyway. It's impossible. Unless you want to go to jail yourself."

He was at the vestibule, about to put on his boots. "You know where my dad is?"

"No. But I know he was brought to the same jail I was. Initially." That was all she knew, and she felt remiss, like she had misplaced Peter's father in some way. "He might not still be there," she said, positive that might be the case. "Have you called your home? Maybe he's there now." She could see from where she sat that Peter had not even considered that likelihood.

His eyes went to her phone. "Can I?"

"You've taken everything else," she teased him.

At the phone, Peter hesitated. "I … I won't know what to say." Whether it was his mother *or* his father, he had a hunch that neither conversation would be easy.

"Peter, these calls have a life of their own. You'll see. You won't have to think much." She watched him dial. At the sound of a voice at the other end, Peter panicked. Agnes could tell he might hang up. She raised her hand, looking frustrated, her signal for him to speak up.

"Hi … Mom?" He heard his mother address him in French, the lilt of her intonation full of anguish. "Mom, it's too complicated." Jeanine's crying made Peter tense up, feeling the burden of his actions. "Mom, I'm sorry. I'm fine. Really." Before she could ask him anything more, he said, "Where's Dad? Is he home?"

He listened as his mother recounted what had happened since he'd left Jamesville. "No, Mom. Don't upset yourself," he told her. "I think I might know where he could be."

His mother interrupted with questions of her own.

"What?" Peter peered at Mrs. Lalande. "Mom, wait. One minute." He asked Agnes, "What's the name of the jail? My mother wants to call some people. She's got contacts in the NDP in Ottawa."

Saturday,
October 17, 1970

Jeanine's calls to the New Democratic Party officials in Jamesville, then Ottawa, had managed to create an impetus for Bob's release. When Peter arrived at the jail, however, the only information he had was, at best, speculative. Agnes's sage advice—to be as polite as he could be—was his internal mantra.

"Hi. My name is Peter Mercier," he said at the visitors' desk. "My dad's being released from here today." He presented his high school ID when asked for proof of identification.

The man took the card and went to another desk. Peter could see the transaction, checking some papers from a stack before making a call. Too far away for him to hear the conversation, Peter stood there idly, finding the provincial prison reception area daunting. His few days with Jean-Louis had made him more wary of the system, but he hadn't realized how much until he was confronted with men in uniforms all around him. Unease set in like a slow poison.

Sergeant Megan picked up the receiver on the first ring. "Megan." He listened. "Make him wait. I'll be over soon." The prison official at the other end of the line was about to hang up. "Wait. Listen, I have to set up a team to shadow them. Can you make up a story to kill some time?" He thought for a second. "Do me a favor. Give the kid a *tour*," Megan said, placing *tour* into vocal italics. "Don't let him know what's going on. Let's scare the crap out of him. Might even teach him a lesson." He waited to see if the guard was on board.

"Will do." The tall man with the build of a bruiser took Megan's suggestion to heart. He used his index finger, as if Peter was a child, to communicate that he should follow him. Their route took them past a series of gates. Each time they crossed the clanking of one locking behind them, Peter's hackles were raised. Then he would remember his mantra, see Agnes's wizened skin in his face, telling him to behave, and Peter would tamp down on his resentment.

At intervals, they would stop, and the guard would walk away, telling Peter to wait there, to not budge. Peter could see the vast complex of incarcerated people, imagining the paucity of peaks and the inordinate depressive valleys of these lives locked away. He had never experienced claustrophobia, but now, catching glimpses of the quotidian behind bars and heavy metal doors, the totality made Peter sick to his stomach.

They had been walking down this labyrinth for what felt like an eternity when Peter lost it. "Is this going to take much longer?" he asked, loath to go any further on this futile quest. "My dad's connected to the NDP, you know. My mom's already called Ottawa."

The idea that political connections mattered in times like these amused the guard, but he could tell their ruse was wearing thin. "Just doing my job. Following orders," he answered. They had walked in circles on three floors, taking the lengthiest of distances to get from A to B, only to arrive mostly back at A again. "Wait there." The guard indicated three chairs that were in a row. "I'll check to see if the paperwork's completed." The guard disappeared again into another office, whose fortified glass door permitted a clear view from inside and out. He was at a desk when Megan walked up to him.

The sergeant signed the document for the guard, then went to the glass door. He made no pretense of studying Peter, sizing him up like he would any other criminal. The unwelcome attention made Peter uncomfortable, enough for him to get up from his seat. He walked around in a miniature loop, aware that cameras were everywhere, that he had not been given permission to move. When he looked again, Megan was gone.

*   *   *

The day had turned overcast, with the sun waning in the western sky. Father and son had barely spoken, choosing silence over terms of engagement neither entirely understood. They had agreed, in principle, to go in search of Bob's car together.

They had emerged from the bus at a Metro station and were considering grabbing a bite to eat when a succession of police cars sped past them, their sirens at a deafening blast. "What crazy thing now?" Bob said to Peter, vociferous enough to be heard by pedestrians rushing to get indoors before curfew.

"It just hit the news," a young man said to apprise them. "They found Pierre Laporte. Dead in a trunk somewhere. Everybody's in a hurry." Bob could hear the fright coming from the man. "Curfew is going to be *real* strict tonight. No one's going to be safe out here. Not now. Not tonight." He drew a line across his throat, showing how real the threat was.

Bob glanced at his watch. Catching the subway to the south shore appeared ill-advised. "We're not going to make it to my car." He could see Peter was unhappy with this declaration. "Son of a bitch. I just remembered. The bastards kept my gun." His release documents had not listed that in his possessions; hence, the forgetfulness on his end.

That his father had brought his rifle to Montreal was inconceivable to Peter, just as much as the news of Laporte's death. He had bargained on neither. Had that been the foolishness that landed his father behind bars? Was Jean-Louis complicit in a man's demise? He was unable to process any of the minutiae; the seesaw sensation was untenable. He thought of bravery but then dismissed it. All he could see was his father's pallor, which was that of a changed man. The rug was being pulled out from under both of them.

Bob saw the hotel sign in the distance. He pulled out his money to count it. "We'd better see if we can afford to get a room around here. Maybe I can work out a deal with the clerk."

Peter thought of disclosing that he had cash from Agnes and Jean-Louis, but the obstacles were too many, the pitfalls too deep.

"How's your French these days?" Bob asked, without an ounce of guile.

Peter watched as his father headed in the hotel's direction. He quickly stepped up his pace to draw alongside him, basking in Bob's admission—a certain kind of defeat for the pater, as Peter saw it. *Worth its price in gold*, he thought gleefully.

*

The shabby hotel room had a smell to it. Bob thought of bed bugs as soon as they walked inside. He pulled up the bedspread to assess but found only clean linens. The neon sign outside their window flashed intermittently into the room. Bob pulled the curtains closed as snugly as he could to shut out the bright shimmer. He took off his shoes and undid his shirt. His armpits were rancid from not having bathed. "Boy, do I smell. I'm gonna take a hot bath." He started for the bathroom when he saw Peter on the side chair, staring into space. "You sure are quiet."

Adequate answers eluded Peter. The elephant in the room had been ignored ever since walking out of the prison. Why should things change now, here, of all places? Peter went to the window. He could tell that he didn't belong here with his father. *How do you tell your dad something like that?* he thought.

Bob had reached for a bath towel. He was about to go inside and undress when he turned around. "You have something to say, say it, Peter. What? You're not tired?"

Bob's standpoint—brash, if not confrontative—

was too much for Peter. He went for his coat and put it on.

"What the hell are you doing?" Bob ran over and grabbed at the coat; then remembered the tear during their tug-of-war back in Jamesville. He let go of the material instantly. "What's going on? Are you daft? There's a curfew out there. A man's dead. Is that what you want? To be dead?"

"I don't care. I don't care if I go to jail," Peter said, knowing full well that wasn't the case at all. As a free man able to walk around the institution, he had detested every nanosecond of his stay in the prison earlier that day. He knew he would die if immured in a cell, even for a night.

"Trust me, Peter. That's not where you want to be. You wouldn't do well in a jail cell."

In spite of himself, Peter retorted, "I can survive."

"Not the kind of stuff they'd do to you."

"How do *you* know?" Peter said it in a vindictive way, even as he hated himself for doing so.

Bob couldn't figure out his son's newfound bravado that suggested a double-edged sword. Was Peter daring to question his jail experience? Or was there more to his opposition? The confusion unsettled Bob. "Son, this whole fiasco's been a big misunderstanding. I'll admit it. I've made some mistakes here." Bob attempted to pat Peter on the back. His son let his coat slip down and off. Bob placed the garment on the bed. "We just need to get a good night's sleep. In the morning, we'll get the car. We'll drive back to Jamesville. We'll all sit down over a nice meal and talk things out. Your mom and me, we'll listen—I promise."

Peter liked Bob's conciliation, but he was reminded of the promises made to Jean-Louis and to Agnes. "Don't you want to know how Mrs. Lalande is?" he asked.

Bob was at the bathroom door, about to slip out of his pants and underwear. "Mrs. who?"

"Agnes Lalande? That woman's house you were in?"

Bob held his slacks in his hands. "Oh yeah, did you ever connect with her son? They used to live in Jamesville, you said, right?" The recollection of Peter's many lies was an unfortunate setback for Bob. "Oh no, I forgot there for a sec. I'm all confused. I don't know fact from fiction anymore."

"I guess we connected."

Bob hung the trousers on an open drawer wanting to air them out. "What do you mean? You guess. She's that Louis fella's mom, right?" Bob was losing his patience over the muddle.

"Yeah, she's Jean-Louis's mom, all right. It's just that ..." Hearing his father speak Jean-Louis's name made Peter happy temporarily. Like everyone might be connected to each other one day. "I, uh ..."

Bob's need to use the restroom made him interrupt the flow, unaware that he had just stifled an imminent confession from his son. "Listen, Peter. It's behind us now. Let's just forget this whole damn episode." He walked over to Peter and hugged him, awkward in the spontaneity displayed. Standing in his boxers, he glanced around the room, as though he was looking for evidence that could not possibly be there, and went into the bathroom, closing the door behind him.

Peter could hear the water splashing from the faucet into the tub. He was too anxious to sit or lie down. He peeked out the window, just as a tank made its way along De Maisonneuve Boulevard, patrolling below. He covered the window tightly, emulating how Jean-Louis had done it back at the house. He unlaced his boots and placed them right beside the door. Back at the bedside, he pulled off his jeans and tossed them on the luggage rack, got under a loose blanket, and fell soundly asleep.

* * *

With no lights on in the stash house, Jean-Louis had nodded off, despite his best efforts, influenced by the darkness all around the living room. The last he recalled was his tightening the grip on his gun and a whiff of Peter by his side. The click near his temple made him jolt.

"One false move." Megan spoke softly, crushing the cold barrel into the skin so that it bruised and bled. He could see the revolver in Jean-Louis's lap and tucked it into his waistband. Out of uniform, lit by the streetlamp that shone in a crest formed by a sliver from the drapes, Megan was more menacing than ever. "Get up. Slowly."

Jean-Louis did as he was instructed.

Megan pushed him towards the wall switch. "Turn it on." The room suddenly became more real for both men. The sergeant uncocked his gun and slid it towards Jean-Louis's lips. "You look pretty enough to fuck; you know that?" He pried Jean-Louis's mouth open with the metal. "I knew this location was going to pay off. Didn't realize the jackpot."

Rage buried deep in his marrow made Jean-Louis react swiftly. He snatched his confiscated revolver from the policeman's belt and tried to disarm Megan, who blocked him. The men tackled each other to the ground, weapons scattering as they wrestled. The tussle rolled from side to side as each man tried to overpower the other. When Jean-Louis spotted the firearm next to Megan's head, he clutched it and struck the sergeant on the forehead, only to drop the gun in the process.

"*Hostie d' con!*" Jean-Louis rose from the floor and retrieved his weapon. He hadn't decided how to deal with Megan, who appeared unconscious, before the screech of tires pulling up in the driveway made him start. He didn't bother to check who was arriving; he dashed out into the yard and stumbled before vaulting over the fence, just as a spray of bullets soared.

Sunday,
October 18, 1970

Bob's snores echoed through the room as Peter waited to make a move. He had been awake for hours, trying to decide on what to do next. He tested the waters by sliding off the bed ever so quietly. With no outward interruption in the modulation of the snoring, Peter tiptoed to his pants, coat, and boots. He snuck out of the hotel room in his stockinged feet.

Coming out of the elevator in the lobby, Peter saw two men in suits. One was sitting, half asleep, with a newspaper on his lap; the other was standing, reading another section of the paper. The distinctive under-cover-cop brand made Peter retreat back into the elevator. He pressed the doors-close button like he had never been there, praying he had not been spied.

He found an unlocked door at the back of the hotel and crept along the side wall, trying to be as inconspicuous as he could make himself. The streets were deserted but for a set of headlights driving his way. He ducked into a tiny space between two buildings until the vehicle had gone by. He waited a minute, came out again, and continued to slink down the street, unsure of how much danger he was courting.

The dawn outside was preening over the horizon, its golden glow reflected in the windows of the taller high-rises in that section of Montreal. At the park in front of the Metro station, he made himself scarce, standing behind a tree hidden by high bushes. He waited to see people walking around and for cars to be back on the streets before he proceeded to catch the subway. The October sun was shining as Peter came out of the station and took the first right, just as he had done a few days prior. The house he had shared briefly with Jean-Louis and the others was easy to find. He made certain that no one was in a parked car along the street, no clandestine activity that could signal trouble, before he walked up to the front door. His spirits were dejected when he found the lock busted, the entry ajar.

Ever cautious, he turned to confirm that no one was following him and walked inside, shutting the door behind him. "Hello? Anyone here?" He waited with bated breath. "Jean-Louis?" he called out. From the corner of his eye, he saw the front curtains flap. He stopped dead in his tracks, his heart beating wildly, for fear of someone behind them. When nothing seemed untoward, Peter advanced slowly to the drapes. Just as he came to pull the material aside, his foot stepped on fragments of glass. His eyes refocused on blood over the floor. He took a deep breath and tugged away the curtain. A smashed pane had icy strands where the inside air and outdoor moisture comingled. Peter spun on his heels, thinking he had heard movement. The crunch of glass under his feet made him grimace.

"You looking for someone, Peter?" Megan's low timbre traveling through the air startled him. He saw Sergeant Megan, in uniform, walk towards him from the middle bedroom, where the firearms had been stored. Without a second's hesitation, Peter made a run for the back door through the kitchen. He sprinted across the yard as Megan chased after him.

"Stop, or I'll shoot," the officer commanded. Megan cocked his gun and aimed it squarely at Peter's back, confident that the teenager would surrender. To his consternation, Peter jumped the fence, like he had done on dozens of occasions in track and field hurdles. The ricochet of a gun firing and a bullet hissing through the air was more exhilarating than anything Peter could have imagined—a fire in his belly from the unresolved his quixotic liaison had brought, which guided him forward.

"Little prick." Megan returned his firearm to its holster and ran to his car.

* * *

The apartment building appeared totally deserted. Peter could see no commotion in any of the apartments and pondered if that was on purpose, if everyone had been evacuated. Was this a known FLQ hiding place that he needed to steer clear of? Peter was clueless, crouched in the alleyway like the fugitive he was. He had come here out of desperation—a bleakness he had not known could exist in the world. He waited until he couldn't wait anymore and scuttled up the three flights of back stairs, hoping his nimble footsteps were inaudible. Peter peered through the window to see if anyone was there, knocking as innocuously as he could. When there was no response, he used his gloved fist to break one of the panes. It was not seamless at all, like in the movies, but jagged. "Ouch! Fuck that hurts." As carefully as he could, he undid the latch and entered the premises, cupping his throbbing knuckles.

Inside the kitchen, there was a scent he associated with Jean-Louis. He tentatively called out his name. The serene calm that remained after he had spoken brought respite on this layer of loneliness. Peter ventured to the bedroom, checking out the bathroom as he went by. There were no signs of rummaging, no indication that the location had been discovered by the police.

Peter stood at the foot of the mattress, remembering his first time having sex there. He resisted the temptation to lie down on the crumpled sheets, certain that he might never bother to get up if he did. Just roll up into a sinking ball, trying to recapture what he was afraid he was losing all of a sudden. He walked to the chest of drawers, opening each randomly. Amongst T-shirts and a sweater, he saw a photograph—a picture of Jean-Louis with longer hair, a younger complexion. *Sixteen, at most*, Peter thought. Jean-Louis's smile was impeccable—a mix of hubris and innocence, framed poetically under bright sunshine and wonderful spring colors outside. His V-sign for victory, all-encompassing. The hint of posterity around the group pose made Peter wonder where they all were today, hazarding a guess that they might have been holed up with them at the stash house. He tucked the photo into the inside pocket of his coat and scrammed.

He traveled the streets, piloted solely by instinct. At the corner where he had stood on his own two days prior, he could see signage in the convenience store window. He crossed the street, ducking as much of his head under his hat as he could as he advanced. *Pour La Révolution* was scrawled boldly with a Magic Marker under the generic FERMÉ/CLOSED sign. That it was out in the open like that gave Peter a sense of security, as though he belonged, somehow, to that insurrection.

Back on Chestnut Street in Saint Lambert, the afternoon had turned overcast. All the leaves that remained on the trees seemed to be hanging on by a thread. A few yards away from 109 Chestnut, Peter saw a car with two men sitting in the front seat. He walked on, pretending his errand was as far away from there as possible.

He surveyed the alleyway around the corner to get the lay of the land. All he could see were garbage dumpsters and trash cans. Access to the yards did not appear to be under surveillance. Down he went, surreptitiously, the length of the passageway, counting structures under his breath, hoping the fourplex was recognizable from the rear. When he arrived at the fence, he found the gate locked from the inside and had to jump over it. He tried the door, which was also locked.

It took a couple of knocks before Agnes answered. "I guess you're a slow learner after all," she told him, poker-faced. She glanced around anxiously before pulling him inside, fastening both the chain latch and the lock behind him. "You look awful." She would have used the word *shit*, but since she had spoken to his mother over the phone that one time, restraint was in order. "Where did you sleep last night?" Peter was already getting comfortable. He had taken off his coat and was about to slip off his boots when she said, "Don't. The place is really messy. Just wipe them down."

He did as he was told. "In a motel. With my dad."

Her disappointment that he had not stayed with his father was apparent. Had she been consulted, she would have advised him otherwise. "Where is he now?" When Peter gave her no more of an answer than a doleful shrug, Agnes sat down at the table. "He's going to give up on you. One of these days." She reached for her tumbler of bourbon. "Have you ever thought about that?" She went to the front of the apartment and came back into the kitchen. "They're still out there."

"I know. I'm not stupid. I saw them. I just went past them. It's not like they have a picture of me somewhere."

"Don't be too sure of that." She was about to pour herself another drink when she indicated the coffee-pot on the stove for him to make himself at home.

"To be honest … uh …" Peter hemmed and hawed. "I could use something stronger. I'm really shaken up here."

She considered his state of mind and the goings-on of the last week and went for the other Courvoisier bottle she kept on the shelf next to the sink. "We're all going to die anyway. Might as well have the good stuff." She brought the bottle and a glass for Peter and sat down. She poured an ounce and passed the glass to him, placing her cognac directly into her coffee mug. She raised the container. "*Santé.*"

The two drank in silence.

"Why do you always think we're going to die?" He could see Agnes was without an answer. "Is it— because of your husband?"

Agnes went to peer out the window over the sink, having seen the reflection off a car hood go by. She saw the parked vehicle in the alleyway beyond the fence. She relocated from the position of vulnerability—a bull's-eye in the making through the window— and leaned against the wall, the early days of her married life floating up to the surface. "You know, loss is like growing old. You deal with it slowly, a little at a time." She studied her hand, using the light from the ceiling fixture. "See this hand."

Peter obeyed, suspecting the drink was taking over.

"How the skin is dry. There's wrinkles, age spots, where once was a beautiful, young hand." She held it upwards, like a slinky model might for a demo. "I never noticed it growing old, though I saw that hand—*every single day* of my life." She sipped. "It's like that—grief. Losing someone you never thought you'd lose. You don't notice it after a while, but you feel it. Every day. Never aware that sorrow dug a hole inside you. Then ..." She clicked her fingers. "Just now and again, a part of you goes crazy. Very quietly. It's from talking with the dead too much of the time."

Her speech was rhetorical, and Peter sat back down.

He appreciated the sweet burn of the brandy against the inside of his mouth, how the liquor swirled effortlessly against his tongue. "How did he die, your husband?"

Mrs. Lalande stared at him, speculating if he even had an endgame in sight. "My Jean-Louis— he didn't tell you anything?" The teen's ambiguous expression gave her reason to doubt him. "Come on, what did he tell you?"

"He said he didn't know. Something about the RCMP."

Agnes looked out the window again and saw two cars now in the alleyway. She moved from there with purpose, took Peter by one arm, and escorted him to the living room.

She sat them down on the sofa and took out a photo album that was on a shelf under the coffee table.

"That's him? Jean-Louis's father?" asked Peter, gazing at a photo of Lionel Lalande in a soldier uniform.

Agnes wiped the plastic sheet over the aging snapshot using the side of her sleeve. "Lionel. That's when I met him. During the war. He had been in Japan."

"Japan?" Peter had left his jacket with the frog back in the kitchen and thought of getting it to show her.

"*Ben oui. Regarde.*" She pointed to an étagère unit in the corner of the living room, right next to the bar cart. The assortment of oriental figurines covered the contoured shelves. "He brought me all of those souvenirs. Shipped them so none would break." She had the gaze of a newlywed embracing nostalgia.

The collection fascinated Peter. He went to peek out the front window first, checking if they were still under surveillance. He saw two cars with men inside them. That he and Agnes might be in the line of fire bothered him. He picked up a couple of the ornaments, picturing them being purchased at the same time as the green frog. "When did Lionel ... get involved ... with ..."

"With the RIN? You've never heard of that organization, probably. Am I right?"

"RIN?" He pronounced it like she had, making a word out of the acronym.

"Le Rassemblement pour l'Indépendance Nationale. It started in 1960. The Assembly for National Independence was there before the FLQ."

She wanted another drink but was too lazy to get up. "Lionel had seen the world. He was in Africa for a while. They sent the Canadians there under the United Nations. He had such great dreams for us."

Peter thought he heard footsteps outside. He went to the window to investigate. The street was empty now. Agnes picked up on his sigh of relief. She invited him back to the sofa to reminisce, a distraction she managed only within the insulation of drink. She turned the pages so Peter could observe photos of the Lalande family—Jean-Louis at varying ages. Peter could see the striking resemblance between father and son. At the end of the book, there was a newspaper clipping. The caption read, "RCMP deny any wrongdoing." Sergeant Megan, confronted by a throng of reporters in the photo, went unrecognized by Peter. Opposite the article was a picture of a massive cortege assembled on the front steps of a Catholic church.

"This was his funeral?"

"Hundreds of people came. They knew he was a hero. That he was martyred."

She had just begun to share the events of that day when Peter noticed a dark spot on the carpet next to Agnes's recliner. From where he sat on the sofa, Peter was almost positive it was blood. He rose to see it up close. The gumminess revealed to him immediately what it was. He turned to Mrs. Lalande, about to drill her for answers, when they heard breaking glass coming from the back bedroom of the apartment.

Peter darted down the hallway into the bedroom to find Jean-Louis at the window, holding a revolver, ready to shoot. "I went all over looking for you," Peter began to say, but a booming voice came from a bullhorn in the alleyway.

"The house is surrounded! Put your hands up in the air where we can see them, and come out. You have one minute."

Agnes had ventured to the door, and Peter confronted her. "What happened? When did he get here?"

The fight had all but left her. Mrs. Lalande barely shrugged before she walked away from the fray, back to the living room, to the pictures in her album, where her Lionel still lived to give her comfort. Peter moved nearer to Jean-Louis.

"Get down," Jean-Louis snapped, indicating with a gesture that Peter do so quickly. "They'll shoot you if they can."

Peter stooped before sitting behind Jean-Louis. "How many are back there?" he asked.

Jean-Louis's pitch was gravelly as he responded, "Three cars. Last time I looked." When Jean-Louis turned, the outside light from headlamps gleamed against a dark, opaque sheen on his shirt. Peter shifted sideways to touch the blotch. "Ow, don't. *Ça fait mal.*"

"What happened? How did you get hurt?"

Jean-Louis had no time for story. "Peter. Listen. It's going to get bad real fast. Why don't you walk out there. Right now. I'll tell them you're coming out. You'll be safe."

"I wanta be with you. I don't want to leave you, Louis."

"Listen, the road's up for me."

Peter made an attempt to move closer, but the other man put up his hand to stop him. "It doesn't have to be," offered Peter. "Why does it have to be? You can give yourself up. It'll be okay." As Peter said this, he could see how flimsy his argument was. All around them, a war was being waged, and he grasped they were mere cogs with no value he could barter with.

"Listen, we don't have time for this. Get out. Now!"

The RCMP officer's bullhorn rang through the night air again. "Your time is up. This is your last chance. Come out now. With your hands up in the air. You will not be harmed."

The room suddenly became quite frosty. "*Ostie, écoute-moi, Pierre. Va-t'en.* This is isn't your cause here."

As definitively as Peter could, he answered him. "*Oui, c'est ma cause.* I'm French, remember?"

"This is your last chance." The bullhorn squeaked noisily as it was shut off.

"Wait!" Jean-Louis yelled. His raspy voice traveled, if faintly, from the broken window. "I've got a hostage in here. I'm sending him out." He took a breath to muster his strength. "He's unarmed. Don't shoot him." He turned towards Peter and bellowed, as ugly as he could come across, "Get out. *Now*!"

Peter tried to hold on to Jean-Louis. The man winced in pain as he pushed his young lover away. Peter looked at his palms, which were smeared now with a gummy coat of blood. He grabbed Jean-Louis one last time, feeling a sickness in his stomach, tasting the wetness of his hair. He ran to the kitchen and back, reaching into his coat pocket. "Here—take it," he said, dropping the glass frog onto Jean-Louis's lap. "You'll need it now, more than me. I want you to come back to me," he said, dashing out of there, a flash of anger mixed with despair.

Outside, by the back door, Peter held up his arms, reminded that this was anything but a game. He walked deliberately down the path to the back gate, where two officers were waiting. They pounced on him, their excessive force throwing him down to the ground. In the struggle to breathe, Peter thought he saw his father peeping at him from the back of an unmarked van.

"This is your last chance to surrender." The

mechanically enhanced voice was more visceral out here. Compared to hearing the commands from within the safety of the house, the screech of the bullhorn carried terrifying authority out in the open air.

Peter heard Jean-Louis yell back at the troopers, "You'll have to come and get me." A gunshot rang from the window into the air. The officers around him ran for better cover, taking Peter with them, as others returned fire.

"You can't shoot," Peter pleaded. "His mother's inside."

The RCMP to his right let go of him and rolled over to the last car, where Megan was stationed. Peter could see them talking.

"Hold your fire, men." Megan lurched to where Peter was crouched, his weapon at the ready.

From the last vehicle, Bob rolled down the window. "Get in the car, Peter. Now!"

"Mercier, this is no time for any heroics," Megan muttered furiously. "Get your damn head down like I told you, you idiot." Sergeant Megan snatched Peter up and dragged him to a safer spot behind a cinder-block garage. "Listen, Peter. Who's in there? I want the goddamn truth now." He held him by the scruff of his neck, choking him. "I know you're involved with Laiande. We've got you placed at two of his hangouts. We've had you under surveillance." Megan could see Peter was paying close attention now. "We have the pictures to prove it. I don't care how young you are. I'll get a judge to throw the book at you. Your little ass won't get to see the light of day till you're forty. You got that?" He let go of Peter, who gasped for air.

"There's just Mrs. Lalande and Jean-Louis." The light from some source shone on Megan's features. Peter stared him right in the eye. "He's been shot, or don't you know that already?"

Megan was tempted to slap the kid, hard, but kept his temper in check, knowing that antagonizing the youth would bring him no results.

"He's in the back bedroom, and he's armed."

"How many guns?"

Peter vacillated. He presumed the guns from the stash house. "Two? Maybe only one," he said.

"Where's the old lady?"

"She was in the living room in front when I left."

"She drunk?"

The characterization, coming from Megan, made Peter indignant. "No, she's not drunk!" He paused to see if that made any difference. "What are you gonna do?"

"None of your goddamn business." Megan considered their next option. He pinched Peter's ear like he was training a dog to attack on cue. "Don't fucking move an inch." Megan ran back behind the cars and maneuvered to the front vehicle, where four of the officers were waiting for instructions.

Peter watched as three of them sidled past the cruisers and down the alleyway. When he thought no one was looking and he had safe passage, he crawled to the open gate, then ran to the back porch, trained for the door.

"You stupid cock-sucking prick." Megan lifted his gun and was aiming to shoot when Bob jumped out of the unmarked van. Megan's only option was to tackle him to the ground. Before the officer could utter a word of recrimination, a single gunshot was heard from within the apartment.

Peter had just stepped into the kitchen when the fiery sound made him freeze on the spot. For a moment, he was convinced he had been maimed. His ears rang and his heart pounded as he inched towards the back bedroom. At the door, he found Mrs. Lalande inside, standing there, gripping the revolver, with Jean-Louis at her feet. Peter rushed to his side. "Jean-Louis ... Jean-Louis," he said. As if the wind had been knocked from him, Peter could not breathe properly.

"Pierre, your face—so beautiful."

Peter tried to lift Jean-Louis into his arms to facilitate communication, but he was too heavy for his smaller frame. The glass frog fell from Jean-Louis's hand onto the floor. Peter reached for it and clutched it to his chest.

"*Pour ton ... propre voyage*," Jean-Louis whispered, a shroud of a blessing on his final breath.

"*Kaeru*," said Mrs. Lalande, with the accent on the letter A.

"*Kaeru*?" Peter repeated but emphasizing the letter U instead.

"*Non. Kaeru*," she corrected. "The accent on the U—it just means frog. But on the A, it means *return*. It's meant for a safe return home. Lionel gave Jean-Louis that memento the night before he went to plant that bomb."

The years disappeared before Agnes's very eyes. She had not been there, only been told what had happened when Jean-Louis returned home with his account of the morning's events. He had described how his father placed the package in the mailbox and how the debris from the littered Canadian mail was all over the pavement. She remembered him telling her the story, all while he held the glass frog in the cusp of his hand, like it was a magic amulet that could protect them all. How wrong he had been.

Agnes placed the revolver on the floor beside Peter. She edged to the other side of him and lifted her son so that Jean-Louis was between them. She kissed him on the lips for a last goodbye. "He's still hot." She thought of the losses she had incurred for the motherland. "He's always been too hot. But never an ounce of mean-spiritedness in his beautiful heart." The idea that he was gone was sinking in gradually. "*Toujours pour la Patrie*," she said, her voice trailing off.

Her tears fell unexpectedly. She never cried, only thought of crying but never did. She and Peter knelt there, holding Jean-Louis's body in their combined grief. From the front of the house, they heard the boom of a broken-in door.

"Put your arms up so we can see them," an officer shouted from the hallway.

The three officers who entered, one by one, into the bedroom, lowered their raised firearms as the scene before them sunk in. Megan and Bob were the last ones to walk in.

Monday,
October 19, 1970

With every officer on call since the crisis began,
the RCMP offices in Montreal had never been so
depleted. Higgins reentered the interrogation room,
this time with a preliminary report from the crime
scene. He sat next to Megan. "You want anything,
Agnes? Coffee? Tea?"

"I'll have bourbon. Straight up," she said, pretending she was in a bar. She studied Megan's
expressionless face. "What?" she challenged him.
"No sense of humor?" When Megan stayed non-
committal, she went in for the jugular. "You're just
like your old man; you know that?" She might have
struck him, the way he flinched. If she closed her
eyes long enough, she could see Douglas Megan's

lecherous gaze superimposed on the sergeant—the shape of the brow mostly, high and flat, accentuated by a widow's peak.

"You can leave my old man out of this," he threatened openly.

Higgins, unacquainted with the familiars, looked at Megan for an explanation. When no answer was supplied, he asked Agnes, "You knew the sergeant's father?"

Agnes mulled over the choices she had to offer. Could she have ever imagined the progression between her sixteen-year-old self and sitting in this chair, in this room? Her faint nod seemed to concur a connection. "He dated ... my mother." The euphemism for her mother's paramours brought up a surliness she had forgotten existed within her. A simmering growl, like a caged animal that had been in captivity for too long, was just below the surface. "He—"

"Shut the fuck up, cunt." The zeal in Megan's verbal assault jolted Higgins.

"Megan." The superintendent tried to intercede.

"When he went back to your mother, did he beat you up too? You were what—twelve? Thirteen? Did he tell you how sorry he was for fucking up? Yet *again*?" A lifetime of bitterness fueled her goading. She had too many questions with missing answers. With her son dead, she had nothing to lose. "Doug probably bragged to you that he screwed me. He was always a showoff. Didn't bother to tell you it was against my will."

Megan laughed, which disturbed Higgins, who saw the man for what he was—a brute. "He said your mom was a whore." His taunting had an almost childlike quality to it, in stark contrast to the subject matter.

Agnes laughed right back at him, a force to be reckoned with. "He was right on that score." She disregarded that he'd implied she was a whore too. The day Douglas had ripped off her slip and panties, Agnes had begged him not to. The speed of the rape, the forcible entry that slit her open, had been painful and bloody, leaving scars deeper than skin permitted to show. The animus her mother had displayed during the following weeks had retraumatized Agnes—a type of disengagement by her sole guardian that left Agnes alone and mystified, that prepped her for her muteness when Dennis showed up in their lives. "Is that why you killed my Lionel? For retribution? My mother fucked your dad. Your dad fucked me. He fucked you and your mother up. And now you want—"

"That's enough, Agnes!" Higgins sensed the escalating tension that could not be arbitrated there. "Megan," he ordered, "let's go."

"What? We haven't finished."

Higgins held the door open. Megan followed his superior into an observation room two doors down, ignoring Peter's reflection on the other side of the one-way mirror when they entered.

"Harry, forget all her stupid bullshit. She's a conniving bitch. We can make this one stick. She'll go down for her own son's murder."

Megan's flouting RCMP protocol, addressing the superintendent by his Christian name, was undercutting his authority—the last straw for Higgins, who was old-school. The pressure the War Measures Act had put on everyone's shoulders, the exigency to produce results, was not enough for the superintendent to proceed with charges against Mrs. Lalande or Peter. "I'll be the judge of that."

"The fucking kid was in on it." Megan's entreaty was nothing, if not steadfast. "We can *prove* that much, just by his locations alone."

Higgins had not seen any sleep going on twenty-four hours. He was too ancient for this needless stress. "Marshall"—he enjoyed ruffling the sergeant's feathers, though the tit-for-tat usage of first names scored no points with either—"Agnes has agreed to *a* story. This preliminary report gives us cover. The ballistics at the house. It's all plausible denial." He threw the file down on the table, irritated with his stonewalling. "Remember that?" His utterance was stated as a fait accompli. "If *she's* fine with it—damn it, Megan—you should be too."

Megan had never seen Higgins pull rank like this. He had a mind to bring up Lionel and was about to when he saw Peter get up in the other room. "What the fuck is he up to?"

"The door's locked, right?"

The men waited to make sure. When they saw a frustrated Peter bang on the door, they resumed their discussion.

"Agnes vouches for the kid. Do you seriously want to put her on the stand and have her say you're lying? With what I know now about your father's connection to her, she'd make mincemeat out of us. Nothing like a solid drunk to spin a good yarn for the prosecution. Your prosecution. Mine."

Megan realized the can of worms that their patchy history with the Lalande clan could resurrect. Pensions and reputations were at stake. He knew his hands were tied if Higgins was not on board for the duration.

*

Higgins escorted Agnes out of the interrogation room. "You're a lucky woman, Agnes," he said, conscious that a debt to her family was long overdue.

"Even under the most trying of circumstances." He opened the door to another room. "And you." Peter looked up, happy to see a face other than Megan's. "You take your dad's advice. Get back to Jamesville. Forget all this dangerous nonsense."

Peter rose from his chair, wondering if he was getting off scot-free, when Megan came into view in the corridor. What fireworks the teenager might have expected never materialized; the menacing attitude from his previous interview apparently had abated.

Peter offered Mrs. Lalande his arm, a show of solidarity as much as respect. He had an itch to be combative with Megan, but Agnes's patting his forearm made him reconsider. "Since curfew's still on ..." He couldn't recall Higgins's name or his title; he had no recourse but to address Megan. "Uh, Sergeant Megan, do we get a car to take us back to Saint Lambert?"

Higgins nodded to Megan in the affirmative. The subordinate walked over to a plain-clothes constable in the hallway to give him instructions.

"Where's my dad?" Peter asked Higgins.

"Had to make a call. Down the hall, I expect." And with that, the superintendent took his leave of them.

Peter could see Megan, seething in the background, and Agnes cautioned, "Be extra careful with him, Peter. He's on a vendetta that can't be bought. The worst kind."

Mrs. Lalande and Peter passed Megan, accompanying the constable, to find Bob. They could hear him before they came around the corner.

"I don't know, Jeanine. He's not the Peter who left home."

"Get him to come home!" Jeanine's unwaveringness had Bob in a corner. How could he explain to his wife what he himself could barely comprehend?

"He's not really on his own here. I've learned that much." Bob could tell that that wasn't going to fly. He had not been married to Jeanine Poirier for all of twenty-five years for nothing.

"Bob. *This* is his home!" Jeanine said, her voice pitched as high as it could be without screaming.

Bob could not believe what he was about to utter. "I don't know about that, Jeanine." He saw Peter with Mrs. Lalande in the distance and gestured that he wouldn't be long. "I think he's found home—of a sort. And with a lot more French in it too." Bob listened to his wife's argument, for that was what they were having now—a row like they had never had before. "Damned if I can figure it out, Jeanine. He'll come to his senses. That's all I can see—for now." His wife would not relent. "Honey, don't worry. He's not—what? Two-thirds French?—for nothin'. A hell of a lot more 'n me; that's for damn sure." Bob was not about to win the battle going any further. "I'll have to call you back when I know more." He hung up, concerned that their marriage might not survive this thorny outcome.

He joined Peter and Mrs. Lalande. "So ... where to now?"

"This lovely gentleman is going to drive us all back to my place." Agnes smiled at the constable, who recognized sarcasm when he heard it. "Your car. It's still near my house, right?"

"*Oui*," Bob answered, comfortable with the only French word he was sure of. "Unless it got towed away."

The dawn light was firmly on the horizon as the police vehicle dropped them in front of 109 Chestnut. The trio stood on the slush-covered sidewalk. Much like on the drive back to Saint Lambert, there was hardly any conversation at first. Mrs. Lalande knew it was not for her to initiate. She looked at Peter to give him the confidence to speak his mind.

"I have to hang around for the funeral," Peter announced.

The assertion was not unforeseen, but Bob still had a tinge of hurt. Mrs. Lalande felt pity for him immediately. "It's pretty depressing in there, *j'm'imagine*," she said, wanting to alleviate any deadlock. The three regrouped in silence towards some sort of consensus. "You're perfectly welcome to stay in the house. Jean-Louis—" She choked up but just as quickly composed herself. "My son would be honored if you stayed here," she said, thinking the father of Peter would have been a friend of Jean-Louis, somehow. "I'll clean up."

Peter walked over to his father and clasped him so strongly that Bob was convinced there would be bruising. "Dad, I can't leave." He became emotional when he added, "I belong here."

"Your mom's not okay with any of this. I'll talk to her some more." His father took out what cash he had left and tried to give him some, but Peter refused. "You stay. Take care of Mrs. Lalande. She'll need you. We'll figure something out." Bob's thoughts were racing, incapable of admitting to himself that any of this was really happening. "Maybe you can learn more French here. Maybe that's what I'll tell your mom. That might make it easier—for her." He smiled at Mrs. Lalande, hoping what he had just said had changed her notion of him. "Sounds like that friend of yours would have liked that too, maybe?"

Peter began to cry inconsolably at Bob's acknowledging Jean-Louis, even if the conjecture was a little wide of the mark. Bob hugged his son back, holding Peter tightly. Once the floodgate had subsided, the two separated.

"I have the phone number for the house. I'll call—in a few days. You can let me and your mom know how the funeral goes. Can't imagine what we'll tell the school."

"A death in the family?" Peter suggested.

Bob had started to walk away towards where he had left the car, days ago, when he remembered. "Mrs. Lalande, you ever heard of an Eric—uh, his last name escapes me now. He was locked up with me in my cell."

Agnes thought for a minute. "Eric Loisier? *Le professeur?*"

"The professor? Sounds about right." Bob realized instantly that he had met someone important to their movement. "You see him around, tell him thanks. I got what he had to say."

Peter's curiosity got the better of him. "What was that?" he asked his father.

Bob took forever to reply. "I won't ever agree to special rights for French Canada. In Quebec or any other province."

"Dad, don't start now," he said, regretting opening a hornet's nest. "Everything was okay there for a second."

"No, it's never gonna be okay, ever again." Bob understood that much. Loyalty to his poor wife, waiting back home for them in Jamesville, kicked in. "And that's—all right, I suppose." Bob's emotions welled, and he mastered them promptly. "I see maybe where I robbed you and your brothers. I gave you my prejudices, from my own experiences." He had approached Peter and Mrs. Lalande so they would hear him as clearly as they could. "And for that, I promise you, from now on, I'm gonna butt out. *Vive* your Quebec Libre. *Vive* your French, all you want. Maybe I was wrong, not giving you the French stuff that you should have had."

His father's conclusions, the ring of finality to them, bothered Peter. "I don't know that that's what I even want."

"But I'm gonna fight you from the other side." The fervor in Bob's inflection replaced all the tiredness in his body. "You go—discover for yourself, our roots. Go for it." The look Bob gave his son was the closest he could come to conceding a hunch, something more complex than he could comprehend at present. "You stay." He addressed Agnes very politely. "I'm sorry I never met your son. I can see that Peter lost a friend." He began to turn away but stopped. "Peter. Make your peace. Do your goodbyes. You have two homes now. I gotta make my own peace with that somehow."

Those were his last words. He walked sturdily to this car, without looking back again. The engine stalled a few times before he succeeded to rev the motor. He made his full turn and headed off towards Jamesville.

The unnatural stillness inside the apartment

spoke of finiteness as Mrs. Lalande and Peter made their way down the hallway. Agnes was glad to see that the furniture, the cupboards, and the closets were mostly intact, unlike after the first invasion of her domicile. With the official cause of death accidental, the back bedroom was no longer a crime scene to contend with.

"Can I go back there?" Peter asked, as they gathered cleaning supplies from the broom closet. "I'd like to spend some time alone before we start."

She handed him a broom and dustpan. "Be careful. There's a lot of blood and glass on the floor." She had poured herself coffee and offered him a cup, but Peter took a pass.

He waited at the door speculating how the sight of it all would impact him. The easterly morning light was full-blown, casting a brilliant shine on the blotchy floor. The incandescence of the glass shards amid dull, dried blood seemed illogical to Peter.

At the window, where the panes had been smashed, he touched some drops of blood with his fingers and licked the gooey texture dispassionately. "*Mon sang*," he said with a smile, as if those words, *my blood*, were part of his very first French lesson. "My blood," he repeated. He retrieved the glass frog from his pocket, together with the photo of Jean-Louis that he had found in the apartment dresser. He stared between the ornament's greenness in the sunlight and the V-for-victory sign Jean-Louis held high. "*Le sang de mon coeur*," he said—the blood of my heart—and glanced at the blue autumnal sky out the window, "beats for *you*—now."

*

That morning in 1961 on Queen Victoria Monday, Agnes Lalande had held her thirteen-year-old close to her chest. "*Écoute-moi bien*, Jean-Louis," she had said to him conspiratorially. In short order, she beseeched her son to follow his father. To not let him put the package inside the letterbox. To intercept, scream if he had to, to ruin everything. She had made him repeat back to her that he understood. "*J' compte sur toi*," she whispered, before turning him around to shadow Lionel.

Even at that age, Jean-Louis thought of himself as grown up. His father had made sure of that. All of the extolling virtues of the RIN had been inculcated into his impressionable mind. Jean-Louis, his dark hair almost auburn under the light, kept a safe distance, so as not to be noticed. That early in the morning, even his footsteps were amplified, palpable, so that he found himself practically on tiptoes in his sneakers, not to be discovered.

Jean-Louis saw the imposing Armory and

thought of soldiers in a citadel right away. The mailbox, by itself on the street, appeared solitary. He was about to run up to Lionel, per his mother's directive, when he saw the look of glory his father had as he turned around to tie his shoelace. The admiration for the cause was too close to Jean-Louis's heart. All he wished, in that singular moment, was to be like his dad.

Jean-Louis was about to join his father, thinking they were in this together, when the car passed him and whisked Lionel away. He rose from behind the bushes that were part of a fenced-in patch of grass and flowers. Jean-Louis had only taken a couple of paces in no specific direction, adrift temporarily in the romanticism, when he was pushed backwards onto the cement by the brunt of the blast.

His ears were ringing when he opened his eyes to the aftermath. Reflexively, he started to walk away down a side street and then another. In his hand, he held the glass frog he had sequestered in his bulky shorts pocket. He rubbed the scalloped edges of the piece, pleased to find no damage there. He grinned like a kid on any vacation day, facing freedom from school, as he headed home, his mission to waylay all but forgotten. His whistling seemed to carry upwards the refrain from a song he had listened to from his mother's record collection. He could hear the lyrics in his head as he whistled onwards. "Valderi, Valdera, Valderi, Valdera, ha, ha, ha, ha, ha, ha ..." The V-for-victory sign was already his.

Epilogue

Andres and I went back to Montreal not too long ago. Mom had died soon after Dad's passing, and on our way from Jamesville to the airport in Montreal, Andres had asked me to show him where Jean-Louis was buried, seeing as how we had hours and hours to kill before our flight back to Bern. After our two decades together, I was surprised by how little I had actually divulged to him of my own October crisis.

I had to think twice, caught off guard by his sudden interest in all that. I, for one, had buried as much of it as I could over the years; toggled variations in my mind to justify what I had lived. But for a few heated sentences spoken by my father, the trajectory of my life would have been—what? It was a mental game I had played much too often.

Encouraged chiefly by Agnes—as I came to call her soon after all of the flux had subsided from the catastrophic loss—I had dutifully returned home when my mother broke free of her reservations and traveled by train to beg me to reconsider. She had been persuasive, up to a point. Mrs. Lalande became like a stepparent, then—got me during summer holidays and often on long weekends when I had earned my own train fare. Never a bus. The Greyhound buses that ran from Jamesville to Montreal had, on a psychological level, become forever verboten.

On that summer day in 2011, I had seen Andres pose the question to me artlessly. But I couldn't help wondering if I hadn't already relayed to him all there was to know. Or had I lied to him? Lied to myself and lessened my role in the sequence of events? Not wanting to concede that if I had not been around, Jean-Louis might have escaped with Claire; he would have lived. I worried, in a moment of self-doubt, that this might have been the case.

"There is no gravesite." I said it with some sadness, not having appreciated at seventeen that gravestones mattered in the chronicles of men— would matter for the mourners who might want to grieve now and again, down the road, seeking that unique repository for their pain. But Agnes had been adamant. No concrete symbols. One martyr in the family had been one too many, she had proclaimed. "We scattered his ashes on Mont Royal. Where he loved to walk."

Had I shared with Andres that I had taken some ashes and made a pilgrimage with Ryan—stalwart Ryan, until he wasn't—and scattered some where the Greyhound bus had picked me up on that chilly, stoned night, when Jean-Louis was about to meet me? Bring my destiny at his feet. I took a chance and opted instead for safety and the abridged version.

As a compromise, though it really wasn't, we went to visit Mrs. Lalande's grave to pay my respects. I had come to realize, somewhere along the way, that without her influence, I would never have aimed for McGill and graduate school. My success was a combination of her and my parents' tenacity. Incidentally, through Jean-Louis.

I was happy to see that the markers were well tended in the cemetery. "I told you she sobered up in the last years, right?"

Andres agreed with a familiar nod. Agnes had proved a wonderful mentor, despite her drunkenness that reached massive proportions on her road to sobriety, so often described in rock-bottom terms by the bystanders to the chaos. Step number nine in her recovery, making amends, had been admitting to me that she had pulled the trigger, not Jean-Louis in an apparent suicide. The official record of accidental death had simply been Higgins's concession to the Lalande legacy.

"You know that you show up in some Google searches, right?"

Andres's words bulldozed me like no others before. I had never dug deep into the online archives, combing for my past. I'd been under the impression that it existed only as classified documents, sealed for a distant future, perhaps, footnotes that belonged to the ages. His statement unmasked his hidden agenda that day in rather bold fashion. "Okay. Andres, you're making me nervous." If my Spanish had been more fluent, I would have protested *en español*.

"How could you get involved with terrorists?" Andres demanded with the kind of poise he might have used while asking to pass him the butter over dinner.

"I didn't get involved with terrorists." My avowal was strong yet weak with merit. I wanted to add that that was why there had been no jail time, no affiliation with our names and the FLQ. Not for me. My dad. Or for Agnes. But that would have been compounding the lies. And now, apparently, unsubstantiated by the deep, dark web.

Of course, Agnes had told me of Higgins's confession. Not in so many words, she had said, but he had implicated the Royal Canadian Mounted Police and

Megan in Lionel's demise; made righteous amends himself in the end. She had gone to her grave, at ninety-two, owning that final, vital truth. The history books would never reveal that we had been freed in spite of our circumstantial guilt. Or, at best, not in our lifetimes.

But did I owe Andres that broader explanation? How could anyone understand where there was no music but that everyone danced? That a beat, heard by only a few, could transcend the sanity and the soul like that. At the exact same time. My *coup de foudre* had been laced with the autumn smells and the first snows. I had tasted love and sex and political tragedy, for that was what I considered Jean-Louis's death. If there was no music, there was, at the very least, a song in our hearts and love that had bloomed at first sight.

About the Author

Tobias Maxwell is the author of two novels, *Thomas* and *The Sex and Dope Show Saga*; a novella, *And Baby Makes Two*; three memoirs, *1973—Early Applause*, *1977—The Year of Leaving Monsieur*, *1983—The Unknown Season*; and a poetry collection, *Homogium*. His material has appeared in, *Balita* and *Mom…Guess What* newspapers, in *The Gay & Lesbian Review Worldwide*, *Worlds*, *LA Edge*, *Art & Understanding*, *New Century* and *The California Therapist* magazines. His one-act play, *The Mary Play* was republished in 2014 by Black Lawrence Press in *Art & Understanding: Literature from the First Twenty Years of A&U*.

Manufactured by Amazon.ca
Acheson, AB

11279587R00127